KATHY GRANT fled to the safety and security of Springfield when her life in New York took a tragic turn. Little did she know that her past would return to haunt her.

DICK GRANT lived only for the day that Kathy would return to his eager arms. Would his passion blind him to her lies and deception?

META BAUER ROBERTS found the true meaning of love when she married Joe. But could their marriage survive his daughter's latest crisis?

BILL AND BERT BAUER struggle to rebuild their troubled marriage, but their young son threatens to destroy their new-found happiness.

———————————

Series Story Editor **Mary Ann Cooper** is America's foremost soap opera expert. She writes the nationally syndicated column *Speaking of Soaps*, is a major contributor to leading soap opera magazines, and is a radio and television personality.

Angelica Aimes, who wrote *Whispered Secrets, Hidden Hearts,* is a well-known romance writer, author of *So Tender, So True, Divided Heart* and *Daughter of Desire.*

Dear Friend,

Whispered Secrets, Hidden Hearts is our third book in the GUIDING LIGHT continuing series. Book 4 is *Revenge of the Heart.*

I thought I would share with you some of our readers' comments on the first two books:

"Just thought I'd write you to let you know how happy I am about the GUIDING LIGHT books."

B.K., Pennsauken, New Jersey*

"I enjoyed the GUIDING LIGHT books and I look forward to the next one. I remember my mother talking about the GUIDING LIGHT soap opera before I became interested in it. I can really get the background from the books and it makes the program more interesting. I work 4 days a week now so I really appreciate reading what I've missed. I wish you could send all the books right away."

L.S.L., Littleton, North Carolina

"Thank you so much for the GUIDING LIGHT books. I missed about 10 or 12 years of the plot over 10 years ago and would like to get the story staight again since the days of Dr. Rutledge and the Bauer family."

J.W.C., Portsmouth, Virginia

For Soaps & Serials Books,

Mary Ann Cooper

*Names Available on Request

P.S. If you missed Books 1 and 2 of this series, see the order form on page 192 which also tells you how to order books in our other Soaps & Serials™ paperback series.

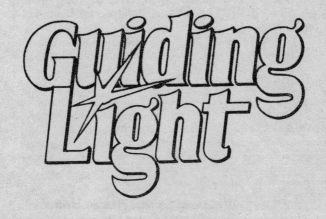

Guiding Light

WHISPERED SECRETS, HIDDEN HEARTS

PIONEER COMMUNICATIONS NETWORK, INC.

Whispered Secrets, Hidden Hearts

GUIDING LIGHT paperback novels are published and
distributed by Pioneer Communications Network, Inc.

For information write to: Pioneer Communications
Network, Inc., 825 Brook Street, Box 5006.
Rocky Hill, CT 06067.

SOAPS & SERIALS™ is a trademark of Pioneer
Communications Network, Inc.

ISBN: 0-916217-03-5

Printed in the United States of America

10 9 8 7 6 5 4 3 2 1

WHISPERED SECRETS, HIDDEN HEARTS

Chapter One

A Lawful, Wedded Wife

Kathy Grant clutched her new husband's hand as if she were afraid she might still lose him. The two of them followed the bellhop down the long hallway, their footsteps sinking soundlessly into the gold and russet runner, creating the illusion that they were walking on clouds instead of on the fifteenth floor of Springfield's first luxury hotel. And certainly Dick Grant felt sky high, clasping his bride's hand with his wedding ring on her finger. He'd dreamed of a romantic honeymoon—making love to his wife on the sands of a tropical island or on a bed of pine needles atop a soaring mountain peak. Instead they were spending the weekend at the Windsor Hotel because he had to be in surgery Monday morning.

The Windsor Hotel was the best and the newest that Springfield had to offer, erected during the building surge that began after the war and was still booming. If the construction continued at the same dizzying rate, the town would have an entirely fresh face by the start of the new decade. It was hard to believe that in just a little over eighteen months it would be 1950. When Kathy left home for the promise and anonymity of New York City, Springfield was still a small town. When she came back three years later, Springfield was fast on its way to becoming a metropolis.

The Windsor was just the newest example of the changes that had come to the town. By local standards, the twenty-six stories of brick and glass made it a skyscraper. The coffee shop and even the formal dining room of the hotel were usually crowded with townspeople eager to taste the elegant fare.

The bellhop inserted a key into the door at the end of the hallway and winked broadly. "The bridal suite!" he announced with a knowing leer. He was just a boy, probably younger than either Dick or Kathy, but his cagey face possessed a worldly knowledge that made them both look like children.

"Thanks." Dick had the tip ready for him. He was anxious to appear sophisticated to his bride, even though he'd never stayed overnight in a hotel before.

"If you need any help, just ring and I'll come on the double." The bellhop winked again and pocketed the change.

Dick looked quickly at Kathy, hoping she hadn't understood the boy's lewd inference. He didn't want anything to mar their wedding night. "Well, Mrs. Grant," he said shyly, when he was sure the bellhop was out of sight and hearing, "I hope you don't think it's corny, but I've dreamed about doing this for a very long time." Before Kathy realized what Dick was talking about, he scooped her up in his arms and carried her over the threshold.

Wrapping her arms around his neck, she nuzzled her face against his. "I don't think it's one bit corny. It's what I've dreamed of, too— more than you can ever know," she added fervently. And it was true.

With all her heart, Kathy hoped and prayed that marriage to Dick would bring her over the threshold to a new life. Her past was a closed book, and no one need ever open it. The time for confessions had passed. Anyway, Dick had never asked her what she'd done in New York. And if he had, would she have answered honestly?

Kathy was saved from admitting the truth to herself by Dick's hungry lips. Easing her gently to the floor, he kept his arms wrapped around her and drew her close.

"I love you, Mrs. Grant," he breathed against the golden aurora of her hair. "I've never loved anyone else, and I never will."

"I know," Kathy said, looking deep into his eyes, until he felt enveloped in their shimmering violet seas. "Because I love you, too. Only you." She whispered back the words she knew he wanted to hear.

"Darling, I want to believe you . . . and I do. I do." His boyishly handsome face glowed with happiness.

Kathy's warm laughter filled the room. "I seem to remember you saying those same two little words not so long ago. We've only been married a few hours, and you're repeating yourself already.''

''I don't know about you, but they're two words I'll never get tired of hearing,'' he murmured between the tender kisses he was bestowing in her hair, along the crest of her forehead, and down the ridge of her ear.

His hot breath tickled her, sending a delicious shiver of anticipation coursing through her. ''You're not afraid of getting bored with me after . . . oh . . . ten or twenty years?'' she teased.

''Never. I'm only afraid of losing you again.''

His lips stopped, suspended above the rise of her cheek as if they couldn't move again or kiss again without her reply. She ran her fingers over his face, tracing each feature—the smooth, ruddy cheeks, the earnest brown eyes, the short, blunt nose, the cleft chin, the waiting lips. ''Never,'' she vowed, molding her lips to his. ''I swear it. You have me now, all of me,'' she added under her breath, knowing even with their first kiss as man and wife that Dick was getting much more than he had bargained for. She had only tonight and tomorrow to make him believe that miracles do happen, and she was prepared to use every trick she possessed to make them a night and day of ecstasy.

She began to kiss him again, lightly at first, and then with greater and greater demand. Her boldness surprised and excited Dick. A low moan escaped from the very depths of him as he crushed her in his arms, answering her kisses with the infinite love and desire he'd kept locked in his heart through the long, lonely years without her.

But just when he began to feel that she was really his at last, she broke free of his embrace. "Kathy!" he cried, feeling suddenly bereft. "What are you doing?"

A deep, sensual laugh rose in her throat. "Undressing, my darling, so we can truly be man and wife." She'd already reached the third button of her pink linen going-away dress.

Kathy hadn't wanted to bring anything of her old life to her new marriage. But the hastiness of their wedding had left her no time to shop for a trousseau. Bob had bought the linen dress for her one afternoon in Paris when they'd been vacationing. When she had tried it on that evening, he'd made love to her in it. He had christened everything he bought for her that way, from necklaces to shoes. Now she was anxious to be free of the dress. She didn't want anything, especially a distant memory, to come between her and Dick the first time.

"But what about out candlelight dinner . . . the champagne. . . ." His voice seemed to get lost somewhere in his throat as her dress slid off her shoulders and fell in a forgotten heap at her feet.

"We'll have a late supper—in bed." She smiled wickedly. "I want you hungry first."

"I am." He breathed with difficulty. He couldn't take his eyes off her as she came slowly toward him, in a white satin chemise bordered in ecru lace. The lingerie at least was new. And she'd chosen each piece with care, selecting pale satins and silks that would be provocative without being too daring. From the expression on Dick's face, Kathy knew she'd chosen well.

"Then help me," she whispered, taking his hand and placing it on the lacy shoulder strap.

Her shoulder was warm and soft beneath his fingers. "Don't you want some privacy? The lights. . . ." Dick managed to stutter. He'd always expected to make love to his bride for the first time through a froth of filmy nightgown and negligee.

"Nothing except you," she murmured. As sure and confident as Eve in the Garden of Eden, Kathy reached up and loosened his tie, then started her languid, seductive work on the buttons of his shirt.

"You're trembling," she whispered as he dared to slip the strap off her shoulder.

Dick had dreamed for so long of the time when he would finally make Kathy his own, that now that the moment had come he was seized with uncertainty. He had loved the girl she'd been when she left Springfield. But what if that girl didn't exist anymore?

"Trust me, darling," she murmured as she stripped off his shirt. "It will be beautiful." She would make it beautiful—more perfect than his most secret fantasies.

In slow, liquid motion, Kathy put her arms around him and drew him into a warm embrace. He took her face in his hands, searching it for the truth he longed for above all else. "Do you love me, Mrs. Grant?" His voice was low and urgent.

Her teasing eyes answered back with an elusive response. "Carry me to bed, Dr. Grant, and I'll let you count the ways."

Her lips were exploring his face, making it difficult for him to think clearly. He'd imagined that he'd be the one coaxing her into bed on their wedding night. Instead, he was the one resisting. With a vague reluctance he couldn't quite understand, Dick glanced over at their nuptial bed, which lay wide and white and waiting to be filled. Then, effortlessly, he carried her over, stripped off the spread, and laid her down on the crisp sheet.

She held her arms up to him, inviting him to make his dreams come true. "I've been waiting a long time," she murmured.

His mouth went dry as he looked at her, and he had to wet his lips with his tongue before any sound would come out. "I asked you a question, Kathy," he repeated, a steely note inflecting his voice. "I'm still waiting for the answer."

"A formal one?" She tried to keep her voice light, but her heart was pounding. This man towering over her, demanding a truth she couldn't give, was her husband. She'd been so desperate to marry him, she hadn't stopped to consider that Dick might have changed. When had the earnest young doctor she'd left behind developed such silent strength? Kathy found herself fascinated, but also frightened. She had so much to gain by this marriage—and everything to lose. "I love you—only you, always and forever. Will that do for now?"

"For now," Dick nodded.

He'd known that Kathy couldn't possibly still be a virgin, yet he'd hoped in his heart that she was. She'd always been his girl. . . . Then, all at once, his jealousy and doubts were submerged in the loving symphony she was orchestrating.

When the last note had quieted, he lay on his back studying the elaborate molding on the ceiling. Beside him, Kathy couldn't help remembering her first—even shorter—honeymoon. One night, to be exact, at the elegant, old Ritz Hotel in Boston. She'd been the shy one that time. But Bob had been patient. Now, she had to use everything she'd learned to bind Dick to her more firmly than the most formal ties of matrimony.

The task she'd set for herself was going to be more difficult than she'd imagined only a few hours earlier when she'd vowed to love, honor, and obey him—and infinitely more exciting. The surging power behind his gentle manner had stirred Kathy in a way she'd never known before. She shivered in delicious anticipation.

"Are you sleeping, darling?" she whispered.

"Not yet." Dick's voice sounded distant, remote, although they were lying so close that not even a breeze could pass between them.

"Good," she responded throatily. Reaching across him, she switched off the light. She knew it was now or never. In the brief night and day that she had Dick totally to herself, she had to win him completely—or risk losing him and shaming her father. If Dick ever discovered that he hadn't married Kathy Roberts, she wouldn't be Mrs. Richard Grant for long.

But all thoughts, all plans, were obliterated as Dick enthralled her with his love. His arms held her with the strength of eternity. His lips burnished hers with a kiss that stopped time and tides. His love engulfed her again and again with its power and tenderness.

At last, Kathy lay back, her golden hair cascading over the pillow like glimmers of sunshine, and she smiled in pure contentment. She was finally safe. She'd gotten exactly what she'd set out to get—and more. People did what they had to, to survive. Integrity and honor were noble sentiments, but they weren't much help when your back was up against the wall. At last, she understood Bob Lang. He'd done what he had to to save his own skin, and now she'd done exactly the same thing. Kathy reached for her new husband's hand.

"Mild, gentle Dr. Grant is really a tiger in disguise. What the nurses at Cedars would give to discover that!"

Overwhelmed by the new hunger that fired him, Dick wrapped her in his arms. He'd always dreamed of Kathy—loving her, marrying her, knowing her in the way that no other man ever would. But a new urgency had taken hold of him. He needed to touch her, to hold her, to possess her. When she'd drawn away from him after their lovemaking, he was seized by a desperate abandon, as if he were utterly lost without her touch. He didn't want to hear about the other man—or men—who had possessed her before. He didn't want to know what she'd done or been in New York. He would never ask, and if she offered to tell him, he wasn't sure he'd want to listen.

Kathy was his wife now, he told himself. That

right, at least, she'd reserved for him. They would put the past, whatever it was, behind them and build a new life together. Yet even as she snuggled closer, he was wondering what other arms had held her.

Dick closed his eyes, torn between passionate love for her and anger that she had given herself before. He felt as though he were in paradise—except that Eve had already given in to the serpent.

Chapter Two

Lost Loves

"Congratulations are in order, I presume, Dr. Grant."

At the sound of the familiar voice, Dick looked up from his lunch and saw Janet Johnson standing beside him, holding her tray. Clearly, she intended to join him. He'd been so preoccupied with his own lusty, yet troubling, thoughts that he didn't notice her approaching. Now it was too late to avoid her. He tried to smile, but the result of his effort was more like a scowl.

"That's right. Kathy and I were married Saturday. But I guess you already know that," he added a little sheepishly.

"Everybody at Cedars Hospital, down to the lowliest orderly, has heard about it. The lovelorn young Dr. Grant, reunited with the beautiful princess of his heart." She plunked her tray on the table and sat down opposite him. "Which is just ducky for you, Dick, but where does it leave me?"

Her question hung between them in the silence like a ticking bomb. Dick looked around the room to avoid confronting Janet directly and quickly returned to his half-eaten plate. Everyone in the hospital cafeteria seemed to be staring at their table. He could already hear the gossip ringing in his ears.

Dick played absently with his beef stew, which no longer held any interest for him. He was tempted just to get up and leave. His lunch was ruined, and he'd lost his appetite. But he owed Janet better than that, he admitted guiltily. If Kathy hadn't come back, he might even have married her one day. Had Janet known other men, too? he thought abruptly. She'd been a virgin their first time together. It hadn't been important to him then, but now. . . .

He tried to keep his mind off Kathy. Dick had hoped that once he got back to the hospital, he wouldn't have time to brood about her, but the opposite was true. He couldn't keep her out of his mind when he was away from her. He wanted her every minute. He'd never imagined the extent of his own passion until she aroused it. But disturbing thoughts intruded on his dreams day and night. He finally had what he'd always wanted. Still, jealousy and uncertainty rankled his inner happiness. Kathy was everything he'd hoped for in a wife, and much more than he'd dared dream of. Yet if she'd belonged to someone before him, she could again. The fear took hold of him whenever she was out of his sight, driving him crazy with love.

"I'm sorry, Janet. I don't know what else to say." Dick fumbled with his napkin, embarrassed. "I hope you don't think I misled you."

Janet couldn't look away from him, although she knew he wished she would. She didn't want to make him feel uncomfortable or guilty, but she had a heart, too—a loving heart—or had he forgotten that?

"I did think I meant something to you," she said finally.

"You did. Of course, you did. You always will. It's just . . . well, you know how it was. I was so lonely when Kathy left, and when she came back. . . ." Dick hesitated, trying to find the words that would make Janet understand without hurting her more. He was ashamed to admit to himself that he hadn't stopped to consider her feelings. "We'd always planned to marry. One thing led to another. . . . It was inevitable, I guess—predestined, almost as if it had truly been written in the stars when we were born: Kathy Roberts and Dick Grant. Try to understand, please, for my sake as well as your own."

"You don't have to explain anything to me. That's not why I chose this table to have lunch." Janet's voice sounded more brittle than he'd ever heard it before. "You don't owe me anything, young Dr. Grant."

"But I do, and I'm not the one who changed my name. It's still Dick." His attempt to lighten the conversation had exactly the opposite effect. Janet looked closer to tears than laughter.

"It just takes a little getting used to, that's all.

The marriage was so sudden. I mean, it was practically yesterday that you were going out with me, kissing me—"

"Please, Janet." Dick shifted in his seat, wishing he were somewhere, anywhere, else, and scanned the room again quickly, hoping to spot someone who might join them. Janet waited, still smoldering, until he couldn't avoid her any longer. He had to look back at her. For an instant, as their gaze locked, Dick gleaned the truth in her dark, sad eyes. He felt awkward and weighted with guilt. She cared for him, truly and deeply, and he'd just been using her—leading her on, however thoughtlessly, to heartbreak. He knew firsthand the anguish of love and loss.

"I'm sorry," he said with all his heart, reaching across the table to touch her arm with the briefest caress. "Truly sorry."

Although she believed that he was sincere, his regret gave Janet little comfort. She shook her head, rejecting everything he'd said. "Why the hurry, Dick?" she pressed. "More than anything, that's what I can't understand. You never gave me a chance against her."

"No special reason." Dick tried to shrug off her question. "We both wanted it, I guess. We'd waited so long. It seemed ridiculous to wait any longer, just for the sake of convention. We had no doubts."

"Didn't you?"

He heard the naked challenge in Janet's voice and saw it reflected even more powerfully in her eyes.

"I would have thought. . . . But it's none of my business anymore, is it?" She broke off abruptly.

Dick's face clouded like a threatening day. Her sly insinuations brought back the worries that had been gnawing at him when she sat down. Janet recognized the sudden change with a thrill of triumph. He'd only been married a few days and already she was sure the first kernels of doubt had wormed their way into his heart. Nothing could confirm her suspicions more. Something was rotten about the Grants' hasty marriage. The honeymoon was over, at least for Dick. And now that it was. . . .

Janet smiled for the first time all day. "I'll always be here, Dick, if you need a friend." Her face softened and her voice purred like the promise of a caress.

"Thanks, Janet, but I don't deserve that."

"Please remember it. Because I mean it," she urged.

"I know you do." Dick pushed back his chair and gathered up his uneaten lunch. "And I will." A dark flush colored his cheeks as he turned away.

Kathy had wanted to get married immediately. At the moment she proposed to him, it seemed absolutely right. But now that he tried to state it in a clear, logical way, he couldn't make any sense out of it, either—except as a kind of desperate impulsiveness. But on whose part? Kathy's or his? He'd been afraid to lose her again. But what was she afraid of?

"Daddy's home!"

Bill Bauer's exuberant greeting resounded through his father's house before the screen door slammed shut behind him. For the first time in months, even years, he felt as if he were on top of the world. He'd never been happier or more confident. This time he was going to make it—they all were.

Bert came out of the kitchen wiping her hands on her apron. "Perfect timing. Dinner's ready, whenever you are." She smiled a greeting, reaching up on her tiptoes to kiss her husband. Little Billy toddled behind her, clutching the hem of her skirt to steady himself, like a dinghy behind a schooner.

"Terrific!" he grinned, hoisting his son high in the air until he shook with laughter. "It smells great. Just give me time to wash up and treat this little guy to an airplane ride," he said, twirling Billy around.

Bert watched them for a moment, just happy that they were a family again. "How was your day?" she asked as Billy came in for a landing.

"You won't believe it! We've been doing so well since you led me back to the straight and narrow that Sid thinks we should open up a second office in New York. How does that sound to you? Can you see it on the door? Bensen and Bauer Public Relations, Springfield and New York."

"Pretty impressive stuff," Bert laughed, caught up in her husband's enthusiasm.

"It is, isn't it," he said more seriously. "And it's all because of you. You made it possible for me—for all of us." Still holding Billy, he enfolded Bert in his free arm and hugged her tight.

"We did it together, Bill," she smiled up at him. "That's the important thing to remember.

And I've never regretted coming home to you."

"Knock on wood," Bill added, rapping on his head.

Bert laughed. In the brutal, stormy years that lay behind them, she'd forgotten how much fun they'd had before his drinking got out of control. Now it was almost like falling in love with her husband all over again.

"Why don't you and Billy get ready, and I'll start putting the dinner on the table."

"Aye, aye, boss!" He saluted smartly. "But where's Mikey?"

"He's over at the shop with Papa. They should be back any minute."

"I've got a big surprise for him, too. Did you see this?" Bill pulled the newspaper out of his pocket and read the headline aloud. " 'President Truman to Stop in Springfield on Whistle-Stop Cross-Country Tour.' I thought I'd take the morning off tomorrow. Mikey and I could go down to the station, just like old times. Remember how we always used to do things together?"

Bert turned away. She didn't want to disappoint Bill, but she'd learned how difficult it was to recapture what you'd lost. Mikey had been hurt by their troubled marriage more than she liked to admit, scarred more deeply than either she or Bill had been. He had been very young and painfully vulnerable when their marriage fell apart.

"We'll see," she hedged, seeking frantically for some plausible excuse. "Tomorrow's going to be a pretty hectic day around here, and you know how young boys are. They've always got a thousand urgent plans. So don't count too much on it. Anyway, maybe it's not such a good idea to start skipping days at work so soon."

Bill was feeling too good to notice the edge that had crept into Bert's voice, and he dismissed her worries blithely. "How many times does a kid get to see the president of the United States? Boy, when I was Mikey's age, I wouldn't have missed a chance like this for anything in the world."

Bert smiled wistfully as she started back to the kitchen. "You haven't changed a bit since then."

"I guess that's what my problem is, when you get right down to it." He grinned sheepishly. "Inside this great, gangly body of mine lives a ten-year-old kid who doesn't know how in the world he's going to get over the twelve-foot wall that's locking him in."

"Words spoken like a true philosopher, which you're not," Bert quipped from the door. "You've got five minutes to get washed, Mr. Bauer, and take Billy with you. He looks like he's been eating mud pies all afternoon."

"Socrates to you, if you don't mind," Bill corrected.

Bert laughed. That was one of the things that had drawn her to Bill when they were still in high school. He could always make her laugh. But their life together since that joyful beginning hadn't gone the way she'd imagined.

They were the best of friends, then high school sweethearts, then bride and groom. They took each new step together hand in hand. But instead of a beginning, their wedding seemed to mark the end of their happiness and the start of the pain and anguish. Looking back, Bert thought they might have had a chance if they'd had the first two years alone together to learn how to be a loving husband and wife. But family problems intruded too soon. And with each added crisis, Bill drank more.

Whenever she had tried to stop him with tearful pleas and dire threats, he'd swear to give it up. Usually he did keep his promise, for a week or a month, until the next family crisis crushed him. For a time, Bert had tried to heap all the blame on Meta, with her selfish behavior and impossible demands. Meta Bauer, the sister whom she had always feared Bill loved more than her. Then, Bert discovered Gloria LaRue. For once, Meta was innocent. If Bill was giving his love to another woman, Bert had to look into her own heart to understand why. Stunned and heartsick, she'd packed up the two boys and left Springfield.

Bert was glad she'd ultimately changed her mind and decided to return to Bill. Each day convinced her more and more that Bill was a new man. He had hit bottom in the last few years and lost everything he'd cared about. He had been alone and drowning in alcohol. Bert wanted desperately to believe that he would never risk losing his family again. He hadn't taken a single drink since he'd come back from the Allan Sanitarium, a special clinic for alcoholics. He was working hard again and coming home every night, loving her and her alone.

It was a beginning—a reprieve. Still, the scars

that marked their family went deep. Learning to trust again was the hardest part. She and Bill had forgiven each other and, in time, might even be able to forget. But Bert worried about their sons, especially Mikey. His brief life had been a maelstrom of domestic fury. She'd wanted him so badly, and when he was finally born, his life was fractured by disharmony.

Bert's deepest fear was that Mikey had been irrevocably hurt—and she was afraid to admit it to Bill. Afraid that if he began blaming himself for Mikey's problems, he might seek solace in a whiskey bottle. He was trying so urgently to make it up to his son now. Maybe all the love and attention would work. Mikey was still young. . . .

Bert had just about convinced herself that Mikey wasn't going to be a permanent casualty of her battles with Bill, when she heard Papa Bauer at the back door.

"Where have you two been all afternoon?" She wagged a finger at them. "Dad's home already and the dinner's waiting."

"Ach, Mikey, my boy, then our timing was perfect, wasn't it?" Papa Bauer tousled the boy's hair fondly.

"You bet it was." Mikey beamed up at his grandfather. "Mom, do you know that Grandpapa knows exactly how many seconds it takes to get home from his shop? He's going to let me take his big watch to school when I go back so I can measure the time that takes."

Bert put her arms around her son and gave him a quick hug. "Your grandpapa knows just about everything there is to know, if you ask me."

Papa chuckled, pleased by the extravagant compliment. "There are a few things I wish I'd learned sooner, Bertha. What's the good of wisdom when you're too old to use it?"

"You'll never be too old, Grandpapa," Mikey objected stoutly.

"I second that," Bert said, picking up a platter of chicken to bring into the dining room. "And now that we've settled that question, it's time for you to get washed for dinner, young man. Use the sink out here, because your father and Billy have probably flooded the bathroom by now."

"Do you think there's room at that sink for me, too?" Papa asked.

"Sure." Mikey moved over quickly. "There's always room for you, Grandpapa."

"Get a wiggle on, you two," Bert called from the dining room. "Chicken fricassee won't taste any good ice cold."

The rest of the family was already at the table when Papa and Mikey sat down.

"Well, kiddo, where have you been hiding all day?" Bill beamed across the table at his eldest son. "Mom says you spent the whole afternoon over at the shop. Do you think you're going to be a cabinetmaker like your grandfather?"

Mikey, who was busy pushing his mashed potatoes into a pyramid, didn't even look up to acknowledge that his father had spoken.

Bert took a drink of water and wiped her mouth deliberately, never taking her eyes off her son. "Mike, your father asked you a question," she insisted gently.

"Dunno," he mumbled, a second before a heaping forkful of potatoes entered his mouth, abruptly shutting off the possibility of further conversation.

For an instant, the grin looked as if it had frozen on Bill's face. Then he shrugged it off and came back punching.

"I've got a surprise for you, Mikey. How would you like to see the president of the United States?"

Mikey's eyes brightened at the idea, even though he kept eating steadily, as if finishing everything on his plate in record time were a matter of life and death.

Winking at Bert, Bill reached under his chair and pulled out the evening *Banner*. "Look at this, son," he said, pointing to the big, black headline. " 'An eighteen-car train, the *Presidential Special*, will roll into Springfield tomorrow morning at 10:30 on a cross-country, whistle-stop tour from Union Station in Washington, D.C., to San Francisco, California.' The two of us could go down to the station to see him. I thought I'd take the morning off work. , . ."

Bill paused expectantly. If only Mikey would give him a chance, they could be close again— the way they used to be before his drinking got so bad and he got all tied up in knots over Gloria LaRue. Funny, he'd hardly thought of her at all since Bert and the boys had come back. And once she'd tyrannized his life, monopolizing his thoughts, dominating his actions, demanding every second of his time. Mikey used to worship him, like a hero. He'd been a real father, then. Now he seemed to be an unwelcome stranger in his son's life, avoided and resented. Bill swallowed hard. So much of his heart, his love, and his hope was bound up in a single, simple question.

"Well, what do you say, Mikey? Do we have a date?"

Before the last words were out of his mouth, Mikey's sullen silence exploded in an angry refusal. "No! I won't go with you. And you can't make me!"

The truth was undeniable. Mikey didn't want him. But Bill couldn't bear to face it. Every time the boy turned from him, it was like being stabbed in the heart. He knew it was his own fault that Mikey had withdrawn. God only knew what terrible fears had haunted his dreams. But Bill was determined to make it up to him now. He looked across the table at Bert beseechingly, but she was as stunned and helpless as he.

"It's not every boy who has a chance to see the president of the United States, Mikey," she said weakly, trying to ignore the bitter resentment that seemed to be shooting out from her son like lethal rays.

Mikey's face contorted with furious passion, and he turned on her as if she were the enemy, too. "I'll never go anywhere with him."

Bill's face blanched, and when he spoke, his voice was tight with suppressed emotion. "Whatever you may feel about me, Mike, I am still your father and I will not. . . ."

Mikey's fork came crashing down on the table. "You're not my father," he burst in. "I hate you! I hate you!"

Little Billy, bewildered by it all, began to wail loudly and refused to be comforted. "It's all right, Billy. Don't cry," Bert crooned softly. "Daddy and Mikey are a little upset. Be a good boy now and finish your dinner. There's nothing to be afraid of." But even his mother's soothing words couldn't quiet little Billy.

Papa Bauer reached across the table and found his grandson's hand. "Mikey, Mikey," he soothed. "We only hate those we really love, because we're afraid they don't care about us anymore. Listen to your brother, he sounds like President Truman's train." He chuckled at the little boy. "Are you a train, Billy, whistling into the station of Springfield?"

Mikey's face softened as he looked over at his little brother. Although he was often impatient with him, he was fiercely protective of Billy.

Still holding Mikey's hand, Papa turned to his own son. "I know I haven't been invited, Willy, but I would like very much to go with you in the morning. I have lived in this country for forty years, and I have never seen a president of these United States yet."

"Thanks, Papa." Bill's words came out in a choked whisper.

"Well, Mikey, what do you say?" Papa jiggled his hand.

Mikey kept his eyes fixed on his plate and shrugged. He still clung to his grandfather's hand, refusing to look at his father.

"That's a wonderful idea, Papa," Bert answered warmly. "Maybe Mikey will sleep on it."

"President Truman must be quite a man."

Papa chuckled again. "Have you heard what people are calling him? 'Give 'em hell Harry.' "

"Maybe so, Papa," Bert replied, "but I heard on the radio last night that nobody in Washington believes he stands a prayer of winning the election—no matter who runs against him."

Papa Bauer's timely intervention had quieted the family storm. Even Billy stopped howling, and they finished dinner in an uneasy peace. Bert and Papa continued to discuss the upcoming presidential campaign, but their talk washed over Bill without his even hearing it. He was too filled with conflicting emotions to notice what they were saying.

Although he was grateful to his father, he couldn't deny that he was angry, too. Papa Bauer seemed to be the only person who had any influence over Mikey anymore. Bill still cherished the special spot he'd once held in Mikey's heart. Now, it seemed as though Papa had filled that place. Looking from his father to his son, he felt a burning resentment. Bill knew he wasn't being fair to either of them. He had only himself to blame. Yet he was neither noble nor selfless enough not to feel bitter.

Mikey was always comparing him unfavorably to Papa, and the worst of it was that Bill did feel wanting beside his father. He'd be the first to admit that he had not become the man Papa was. Then and there, Bill vowed to win back his son's love. He would prove himself to Mikey, no matter what price he had to pay in personal sacrifices or suffering.

31

Chapter Three

A Blessed Event

"Sorry I'm late, Kathy. I know you asked me to try and get home early tonight, but I had an emergency—"

Dick stopped dead at the door and stared. All his speech and movement ceased. Kathy had always been beautiful in his eyes, but tonight she was literally stunning. Tiers of gossamer chiffon in deepening shades of orchid seemed to float around her like an evening cloud. One round, golden shoulder glowed naked in the Grecian style. Her cheeks and lips gleamed a deep rose pink. Her long, fair hair was piled on top of her head, forming a crown of soft curls. Two tiny purple orchids rested in them.

Whistling in admiration, Dick circled her slowly, taking in every detail, down to the shimmering silver evening slippers. "To what do I owe this divine apparition, Mrs. Grant?" he asked in awe.

Every plane and contour of her face shone up

at him. "Do you really like it, darling? You're not just saying it to make me feel good?" Her long, dark lashes fluttered and fell, sheltering her violet eyes from his scrutiny.

"Don't I sound like a man who's seen a vision? You look so rapturous, you take my breath away—like a goddess."

"If I thought it would have the same effect, I'd wear this dress every night," she warned.

"I can't think of anything I'd like better—as long as you don't hold me responsible for the consequences," he whispered over her shoulder.

"Is that a promise I can hold you to, Doctor?" she countered wickedly.

"I have a lot more than a promise to hold *you* to," he murmured thickly, as his arms snaked around her waist. Pressing her tightly against him, he drew a line of fire with his lips, starting at the nape of her neck and extending with increasing fervor to the curve of her bare shoulder.

Kathy pulled away before retreat became impossible. For an instant, the only sound was Dick's heavy breathing.

"Where do you think you're going?" he finally managed to ask.

"Not I, silly, we," she corrected. Her laughter rang in his ears like crystal.

"I know where we're going," he insisted, reaching out for her again. But she eluded his grasp.

"Oh, no." She shook her head. "It's too late for any of that. It just so happens, Dr. Grant, that I'm taking you out to dinner at the most expensive, most exclusive restaurant in Springfield."

"May I ask what the occasion is?" he inquired.

"I have my reasons," Kathy answered mysteriously. "Now hurry and change. I put out your dark suit."

"Will you help me?" Dick smiled mischievously.

"Not on your life. I don't dare." Kathy floated by, teasing his lips with a fleeting kiss. "We're late already. And they won't hold the reservation forever—not even for a goddess and her divine escort."

Dick tried to give himself up completely to the mood that Kathy was creating. And, for a while, he succeeded. She was radiant and warm, exuding promises of raptures to come. Subtly mysterious, teasing and tempting, she was his, all his, now. The understated splendor of the restaurant, the soft candlelight, and the romantic music created a perfect setting for Kathy.

He watched her play him skillfully, pulling his strings like a master puppeteer. Yet he was helpless to resist. Love made him easy to toy with. He was vulnerable to her slightest caprice. Inevitably, though, a primitive instinct of self-preservation intruded, directing him to strike back before he abandoned himself irretrievably.

Kathy was leaning across the table, a spoon of meringue glacé poised in the air between them. The outline of a kiss caught on her moist lips. He reached over and brushed it away roughly with his thumb.

"Is this the way you acted with the man—or

men—you saw in New York, Kathy?''

His voice was as dry as the wine they'd just finished. He regretted his words even as he spoke them, and the tormenting doubts that festered behind them. Dick had decided on his honeymoon to block out the past. Now, at the first opportunity, he was letting it come between them.

For a time so brief that it could be measured only by the speed of light, the glow in her eyes faded, leaving them dull and flat. Then it flickered on again, and she caught his hand. The smile that had momentarily frozen on her lips melted and spread, wreathing her face in its warmth.

''I'm trying to decide whether to blurt out my secret now, or wait until you dance with me and then give you three guesses,'' she mused, dismissing his question without a word in reply.

''Let's dance,'' he said, pulling her up with him, ''and you can whisper sweet nothings in my ear, and tell me you forgive me.''

She melded in his arms in perfect harmony, and as they glided across the floor he admired the picture they made together in the long, gilded mirrors.

''When are you going to tell me your secret?'' he murmured against her cheek. ''Or do you intend to hold me captive here until the stroke of midnight?''

''You're the captivating one in this family.'' Her voice was like the contented purr of a feline. ''But I don't think I want to tell. I'll give you three guesses instead.''

''You love me, and you love me, and you love me.''

Kathy giggled. "A triple yes. But that's just about the worst kept secret in the world."

He pressed her tighter in his arms, inhaling the intoxicating perfume of her body. "I guess I'm not very good at playing games."

"You were close."

"But no cigar?"

"Not for a while yet," she laughed. "But it's not such a bad idea to stock up."

Dick shifted her in his arms so that he could look into her face. "What are you talking about darling?"

"Just that . . ." Kathy stopped and lowered her eyes almost shyly, "I'm not the only one who loves you. *We* love you—or we both will in about nine months."

Dick's grip on her arm tightened so much that she gasped in alarm, but he didn't even notice. Although the music was still playing, he had stopped dead in the middle of the floor. "Are you saying what I think you're saying?" he gasped, thunderstruck. "You're going to have. . . ?"

Kathy was nodding so much that her head felt as if it were bobbing like an apple on a string. "It's still early. The doctor thinks about six weeks, but he's sure. I went this morning."

"You mean I'm going to be a father?" Dick shouted. His usual restraint was gone, and completely forgetting where he was, he picked Kathy up and twirled her around in circles. At his ecstatic outburst, the other diners in the usually low-key restaurant gave them a resounding hand. Flushed with happiness, Dick led Kathy back to their table as if she had suddenly been transformed into a fragile china doll.

"Champagne—the best you've got in the cellar," he waved to the waiter. "Nothing but the best for my son, or daughter. Which do you think it is, darling?" He studied her still slender figure intently, as if he possessed X-ray eyes.

Kathy pulled him down into his seat. A deep crimson flush stained her cheeks. "You're making a spectacle of yourself, Dick," she whispered tensely. "Everybody's watching us." Her eyes darted nervously around the room, as if half-expecting someone to challenge her news, but Dick was too excited to notice her trepidation.

"Great! Terrific! I feel like going up to the roof and shouting it to the world. I want everybody to know. We have to think of a name—two names, I guess, one for a boy and one for a girl. But what if it's twins?"

Kathy held a silencing finger to Dick's lips. "Slow down, Doctor. Don't you think you're rushing things? It's still a little early to be making plans."

"What's the matter? Is something wrong? Don't you feel well?" The anxious questions poured out in a burst of concern.

All Dick's doubts and fears about Kathy's past were buried beneath his joy over becoming a father and making a family with Kathy. He'd always thought of her as a girl—his girl. But tonight, for the first time, he realized that she had become a woman, possessed of a woman's awesome power and infinite wiles. At first, he'd resented the change. He wanted Kathy to be his girl forever. But now, sharing her secret, he believed that he understood the change in her. The mystery—the miracle—of life had made her a woman. Nothing else.

"Nothing's wrong, and I've never felt better," Kathy answered defensively.

"Six weeks, you said?" Dick calculated quickly in his mind. "That means it must have happened on our honeymoon. Not bad for a weekend, Mrs. Grant." He grinned proudly. "What do you think it means? Decades and decades of happy, fruitful years ahead, and dozens of children?"

Kathy laughed, caught up in his boundless euphoria. "I'd just as soon take them one at a time, if it's all right with you."

Dick laughed. "And to think I was afraid you were going to declare your independence today."

"From you?"

He nodded.

"Never," Kathy vowed.

"Well it is the Fourth of July weekend, you know. Let's see . . . June, July. . . ." He began to count on his fingers. "We may even have a Valentine baby. Have you told anyone yet?"

"Not a soul. I thought you should be the first to know."

"Well, what are we waiting for?" Dick exclaimed, gulping the icy champagne. "We'll cable Mom and Dad. Do you think we can still catch them in Paris? Or maybe I should send cables to London, and Vienna, and Athens, too. Then one of them will be sure to reach them."

"You're crazy, Dick Grant. Do you know that? And to think you've kept it hidden so well. Why don't we just wait until your parents get back from Europe? After all, it's only three more weeks, and it would be much nicer to tell them in person."

"OK, then let's go over and tell your father and Meta."

"Do you have any idea what time it is? It's after midnight."

"Then we'll call. There must be a telephone around here some place."

Kathy shook her head. "And wake them up out of a sound sleep? You should stop and listen to yourself, Dr. Richard Grant. You've been babbling along like a brook for the last half hour, and not making a darn bit of sense. Since you're a doctor, I expected you to take a natural, everyday event like this in stride. We're going over to my father's for dinner tomorrow night, if you think you can contain yourself that long. I know I can, but I'm not so sure about you anymore."

Dick grinned impishly. "Neither am I. You've made me happier than any man has a right to be," he admitted tenderly, gazing ever deeper into the violet pools of her eyes.

Dick saw the mist reflected in them, but he mistook it for tears of joy.

"Will you let me tell them in my own way, Dick?" Kathy begged as they started up the flagstone path to her father's front door.

He was even more eager than she to break the news to Joe and Meta. She didn't know how she'd expected him to react, but she found his unadulterated joy disconcerting. What if something went wrong?

Overhead, the sky was brushed with twinkling stars and a new moon, scarcely more than a yellow splinter in the sky, hung low over the gambrel roof. Dick breathed deeply, filling his lungs with the warm, clear air.

"Of course. Anything you like," he promised easily, taking her arm. But they no sooner got through the door, than he blurted out their secret.

"How do you think Kathy looks? Notice anything different about her?" he asked pointedly, as Meta pushed Joe to the door to greet them. He'd been confined to a wheelchair since suffering a heart attack a few months before.

"She always looks good to me," Joe answered, experiencing the rush of love and pride that filled him every time he saw his daughter.

"Dear Daddy," Kathy laughed. "How do you feel?"

"Never better, now that you're here."

"Don't you see anything?" Dick blurted again. "Maybe a little bulge?" he added, patting the flat plain of her belly.

Kathy frowned at him in irritation. So much for promises. "What Dick is trying to say in his usual unsubtle way is that I'm pregnant." She delivered the news swiftly in one long breath and waited warily for the words to penetrate. She hoped they'd just accept the news at face value, because she didn't think she could bear up under close scrutiny. She trusted her father to accept it unquestioningly, but she was afraid of what Meta might say.

For a moment, Joe hesitated, stunned and strangely saddened by the news. Until that moment, he could harbor the comforting illusion that Kathy was still his little girl. Now he had to relinquish it. He had given her away to another man irrevocably. She was undeniably a woman, and soon he would see the evidence with his own eyes. He held out both hands to his daughter, who, all at once, had become a beautiful and beloved stranger to him.

"Will you mind terribly being a grandfather, Daddy?" she asked, searching his face for the honest answer.

"Mind?" He caressed the silken hair that fell over her shoulders. "I'll be out of this darn chair in nine months so I can wheel my first grandchild all over town in the carriage to show him off. And that's a promise."

"You'd be up and around a lot sooner than that if you kept up your therapy," Meta responded warmly. "Just ask your doctor if you don't believe me." She shot a compelling look in Dick's direction, as if warning him to back up her claim.

"A grandchild is the best therapy I could prescribe." A mile-wide grin seemed to be fastened permanently on Dick's face.

"I'll drink to that," Joe beamed.

Nothing could have made Joe happier than this blessed news. Ever since Kathy had come back to Springfield, he'd worried that she might bolt again without warning. He hadn't confided his secret fear to anyone, not even to Meta. And now, he could dismiss it forever. With a baby to care for, Kathy would be firmly anchored at home. All the grief she had caused him was obliterated in the happy anticipation.

Meta's response was more tempered. Although she couldn't admit it to them, she didn't feel old enough to be a grandmother, or even a stepgrandmother. She was still young—in the prime of her life. Look at her brother Bill. His youngest was still a toddler. It didn't seem fair.

When Chuckie died, Meta had never wanted to have another child. The very thought of it seemed to defile the memory of her adored son. But when she'd married Joe, she'd harbored a secret hope, unvoiced even in her own mind, that with time they might have children. Kathy's disappearing act had dashed that dream. Not only did Joe abandon Meta on their honeymoon to go in search of his daughter, but by the time he finally returned from the fruitless chase he was too broken emotionally and physically to ever be able to fulfill her deepest wish. Now, instead of her own baby to ease the pain that still gnawed so many months after Chuckie's death, she was going to have a grandchild. She wasn't ready yet to play that role. It was a cruel twist of fate.

Although Meta tried to muster sufficient enthusiasm for Joe's sake, she was afraid the effort was as obvious as a petticoat hanging below a stylish skirt. She was fond of Dick and touched by the unabashed pride that made him literally swell.

"With parents like you and Kathy," Meta smiled," and a grandfather like Joe, how can the baby be anything but bright and beautiful?"

"I hope he's a fighter—honest and courageous and strong—just like you, Daddy," Kathy blurted out. The way she said it made it sound almost like a prayer.

Meta was shocked that Kathy had addressed her passionate remark to her father instead of her husband, and she glanced quickly up at Dick to see if he'd been hurt by her words, implying as they did that he was the lesser man. Why would Kathy go out of her way to slight him publicly when he was so clearly overjoyed at the prospect of becoming a father? Meta studied her stepdaughter curiously. On close scrutiny, Kathy appeared wary and on edge, reminding Meta of herself a lifetime ago when she had discovered that she was pregnant by a man she'd grown to detest.

It was an old and ugly story. When Meta had gone to New York as a naive, small-town girl she'd been seduced by the power and glamour of the unscrupulous Ted White, her boss at the modeling agency. She discovered too late the viciousness and deparvity that marked his true character. For by then she was carrying his child.

Meta did everything she could to protect herself and her young child, but to no avail. When he was only seven, Chuckie died, the victim of his father's possessive cruelty. Meta, half-crazed with bitterness and grief, had avenged her son's death. The memory came back sharply, blotting out the present with its intensity. Her finger squeezed on the trigger again and again, and she heard the flat retort of the gun emptying into Ted's helpless body.

"Meta! Meta!"

The persistent sound finally broke through her memories, forcing her back to the present.

"Where have you been?" Joe's clear, steady eyes were fixed on her with unnerving intensity. "You looked like you were a million miles away."

"Not a million miles, a million years," she responded with a shaky smile.

"Daddy wants to know what you think of Joseph Richard Grant, if it's a boy," Kathy said.

"Quite a name to bear with honor, if you ask me. But Joe, I hope you didn't suggest it yourself."

They all laughed. "Of course he didn't. It was really Dick's idea—I think he's a mind reader," Kathy added quickly.

"You probably dropped a broad hint every other second, knowing you," Joe teased.

"Better Kathy than you," Meta quipped. "Well, Dick, I guess you're discovering fast what it's like being married to a Roberts."

"And loving every minute of it." Dick answered Meta, but his eyes were filled with Kathy.

Looking from one to the other, Meta tried to deny her own intuition. Why couldn't she just be happy for Dick and Kathy, and happy for Joe, instead of looking for trouble where none existed? Dick wasn't Ted White and Kathy wasn't Meta Bauer. They were the perfect couple, and they would have a perfect baby, she told herself with conviction.

But in her heart, Meta distrusted such perfection. It was always too good to be true.

Chapter Four

Fathers and Sons

Mikey sprawled on the living room floor beside the cumbersome console radio, his head pressed close against the outside of the speaker. Above him, the big dial shone coppery gold, like a halo.

"Who knows what evil lurks in the hearts of men? The Shadow knows!"

Across the room, Bill slouched on the couch behind the Sunday paper, watching his son. The only visible part of him were his long legs, which were crossed at the ankle and sticking out into the center of the room. The only sound was the radio voice:

"The Shadow, who aids the forces of law and order, is, in reality, Lamont Cranston, wealthy young man about town. Years ago in the Orient, Cranston learned a strange and mysterious secret, the hypnotic power to cloud men's minds. . . ."

With an inaudible sigh, Bill raised the paper higher and turned back to the classified ads he'd been studying. Mikey had slunk into the room without even acknowledging his father's presence, and Bill knew he would escape the same way the instant the *Shadow* was over. There was no point in even trying to engage his son in conversation, Bill admitted to himself. He had to find some other way to regain his respect and love.

Mikey wriggled even closer to the console, as if the degree of nearness brought him closer to his invisible hero.

"Anything interesting in the paper?" asked Bert as she came down the stairs, fanning herself. Billy was settled in bed for the night. The dishes were done. It was the time of the day when she had a few minutes to relax without a dozen interruptions. She crossed to the open window, trying to catch the slightest breeze, and paused for a moment to look out into the thickening darkness. The street was deserted. The town was shut in safely for the night.

It had been a sweltering day and, so far, the evening had brought no relief. The whir of the large fan in the corner was almost completely drowned out by the blaring radio, which Mikey had turned up to its full volume. Bert went over and stood in front of the fan, holding out the scooped neck of her yellow cotton blouse to allow the cool air to blow under her clothes. Though light, they felt like armor.

"I haven't really read it yet," Bill muttered, still intent on his perusal.

"Well, for someone who hasn't read it, you certainly seem lost in its contents. What are you reading, anyway?" Sinking into the easy chair beside him, she picked up the Sunday magazine and began leafing through it idly.

"The want ads."

Bert stopped abruptly and looked up at her husband. Incipient panic gripped her heart even as she told herself to stay calm. Had Bill and Sid had a fight? Was business skidding to a standstill again? She'd thought Benson and Bauer was doing well. Just a few weeks ago, Bill was boasting about how good business was. Yes, she remembered it exactly; it was when he was trying to get Mikey to see President Truman with him.

"Is there something you haven't told me?" she questioned, trying to keep her voice on an even keel.

"You know I always tell you everything, honey." Bill's pat response just annoyed her.

"For heaven's sake, put that paper down and tell me what's going on," she said in exasperation. "Why are you reading the want ads? Are you looking for a job?"

"I always said you had a brilliant mind, honey." He folded back the paper, then doubled it over and marked an ad with his pen.

Bert was in no mood for his teasing. "I thought you told me that Benson and Bauer was doing better than ever."

"It is. So there's nothing for you to worry about."

"What are you talking about then?"

Bill glanced at his son and caught Mikey watching them. Immediately, the boy turned away, and before Bill could say a word Mikey raced out of the room and up the stairs, as silent as the Shadow and almost as invisible.

"Be sure you take a good bath," Bert called after the retreating figure.

A new show began on the radio, and although they weren't listening to it, neither Bill nor Bert moved to turn it off.

"I'm going to get a second job, Bert," Bill said finally. He saw the protest register instantly on her face and added, "Now don't say a word until you hear me out. I have to do this. You've been like the Rock of Gibraltar to me. You know I couldn't have made it back on my feet without you. I love you, and I love my boys. But I can't do what I want for any of you, because I feel . . . I can't put it into words very well. I feel, well, crushed—both emotionally and financially. When I was drinking and . . . and all," he said, reluctant to bring up the still sensitive topic of Gloria LaRue, "I borrowed every cent I could get. Now those debts are like a great weight around my neck, pulling me down. I never told you this, but Papa gave me all his savings to send to you and the boys in Arizona. And Meta never refused me, no matter what amount I came begging for. I could see in her eyes that I was tearing her apart by asking. She thought she was helping me destroy myself, and on the other hand, she couldn't bring herself to refuse me. God! I'm so ashamed whenever I think of how I acted then. I have to pay them back if I'm ever going to have any pride in myself again. Every last cent—especially to Papa."

He looked hopefully to Bert for approval. "There's a job here for a night watchman. I could go to it when I leave the office and still be home by midnight."

"It's too much, Bill. You'll be exhausted," Bert objected. "Papa and Meta don't want you killing yourself for them. I'm sure if you talk to them, they'll say you don't have to repay them right away. We can put a little aside in a special account every week."

"I have talked to them. They both said they don't need the money," he admitted.

"Well, then. What are we going on about?" Bert smiled with relief. If Bill took a second job, the pressure would be enormous. And if the pressures built, so too would the temptation to ease them with a drink, and then another.

"I'm not doing it just for them, Bert. You don't understand. I'm doing it for us, too. I have to earn your respect and trust again."

"You already have," Bert insisted.

"No. I can see on your face you don't trust me. You're afraid if I try to work two jobs, I'll begin drinking again. You think I'm still weak, and when things get tough, I'll crumble."

"That's not true," Bert protested. But her lie was transparent.

She looked away, embarrassed, but he reached for her hand. "It's not just for us, Bert," he said softly. "It's for Mikey, too. I destroyed his love, and I want to make it up to him. Maybe if I do this, I'll stand tall in my son's eyes again. I don't know what else to try."

"You don't have to prove anything to anyone," Bert insisted. "We're all so proud of the way you stopped drinking, and proud of the way you're rebuilding our lives. For the first time in so long, we're a family again. That's the

most important thing. Please don't do anything—for whatever noble motives—to jeop-
ardize that."

"And Mikey?"

"He'll come around in time, with enough
patience and love. I'm sure of it."

Bill shook his head. "I've been fooling myself
with that line for months. I can't anymore."

Bert frowned. "I wish one of you would tell
me what happened when you went to see the
president. You've been morose ever since.
Mikey has barely spoken a word to either of us.
And even Papa becomes reticent if I bring it
up."

Bill sighed. "Christ, Bert, how many times do
I have to tell you? Nothing happened. Absolutely
nothing. That's what was so awful. If he'd only
scream at me, or hit me. At least I'd know he
cared enough to hate me. But this silent
treatment, as if I don't even exist, is killing me."

He closed his eyes, but instead of erasing the
memory, it flooded back in a sudden rush of
detail: the gray, wet weather, an omen of what
lay ahead; the red-white-and-blue bunting
hanging limply from the station door like a
ruined party; Papa's relentless bonhomie, so
incongruous in the spoiled day; and that brass
band playing listlessly, pausing every few
minutes to empty the water from their
instruments.

"The Battle Hymn of the Republic" was one
of Bill's favorite songs, but after fifteen
renditions, each one worse than the one before,
he never wanted to hear it again. The *Presidential
Special* was a hour and a half late, enough to

dampen even the highest spirits on a sunny day. But in the pelting rain, huddled under the circle of a black umbrella, Bill found the delay debilitating. Mikey refused to get under the umbrella with them. He stood alone, silent and stiff like a wooden soldier, with his eyes fixed on the empty curve of the track. Not even Papa could coax him under.

Though never spoken, the reason was perfectly clear. Mikey couldn't bear to be that close to his father. Bill was sure. Others at the station, feeling sorry for the little waif, offered him shelter under their umbrellas, but Mikey refused. Rain pelted him. It plastered his hair to his head like a cap and drenched him through to the skin. His shoes filled up like wells. But he was too stubborn, or too unforgiving, or simply too young to give up his solitary stand.

When the train finally whistled into the station, it no longer mattered. Bill couldn't even remember now what the president had said. He remembered that Truman kept taking off his thick glasses to wipe them dry as he spoke. He remembered the strong, compelling voice tinged with a nasal twang. Most of all, he remembered the rain washing his son's smooth cheeks like tears.

Bill's grip tightened on Bert's hand, but he didn't look at her. "I can't wait any longer. I'm not a patient man. I'm going to apply for the job tomorrow."

A shadow fell between them. But this one was all too visible and cold.

Monday promised to be another scorcher, even

hotter than the day before. Dick liked the heat, but he worried for Kathy. The heat made her desperate. The only thing that brought her any relief was sitting in an ice-cold bath. He wished he could take her up to the mountains, to a cold, crystal lake, but he had too many seriously sick patients to escape now, and he was afraid to let her go alone. She was getting big faster than he'd expected. Maybe in a week or two, he kept promising.

It was only eight o'clock, but already Cedars Hospital was a hive of activity. Behind him the floor nurses pushed stretchers and wheelchairs toward the elevators, taking patients up to the operating room or down to the labs for tests. Orderlies passed with carts of fresh sheets to change the beds. The buzzer at the nurses' station rang insistently, but there was no one there to answer it. Cries of pain drifted down the hall, carried on the breeze that billowed the curtains at the far end of the corridor. Mornings were always the busiest time at Cedars Hospital. Dick breathed in the familiar hospital smell; alcohol, antiseptic, cleaning fluids, and vitamins melded into one peculiar odor.

"Dr. Grant. Dr. Grant. You're wanted on the telephone." The nasal voice of the page echoed through the hospital halls.

Dick started to go the desk, then checked himself. It was for his father, not him. He'd almost forgotten. This was his father's first day back, after a month-long vacation in Europe. Instinctively, Dick tensed at the thought of having his father back at the hospital. The long absence had been a vacation for him as well. He hadn't sent cables to any of the cities after all, deciding at Kathy's urging to wait and break the news himself.

Dick tried to concentrate on the charts he was reading. He'd make his rounds first, then look for his father. Dr. Richard Grant, Sr., was not a difficult man to find. He was usually very much in evidence around Cedars Hospital. But the voice booming at him from the other end of the hall changed Dick's plans abruptly.

Dr. Richard Grant, Sr., careened down the corridor like a battleship in full sail. His tortoise-shell glasses were angled on top of his head, and a stethoscope dangled from a pocket of the white coat that flapped at his heels.

Dick's father had a prosperous, self-indulgent look. He was a big, booming man whose face reddened explosively in anger or amusement and whose thick, beefy fingers performed delicate miracles of surgery. Dick respected his father as a doctor—but he wished he could do it at a distance, instead of at the same hospital. Beyond that, little love was lost. They had nothing in common except their chosen profession.

Physically, Dick was much slighter than his father. Although he was six feet tall, he had the slender build and small, even features of his mother. In temperament, too, they were very different. Dick had been a quiet, shy boy, always overshadowed by his forceful, aggressive father. As a man, he was restrained and reticent, and still overshadowed. For a while in college, Dick had almost convinced himself not to study medicine. He didn't want to have to compete with his father. But in the end he went on in spite of his dad, because being a doctor was the only thing he'd ever wanted to do with his life.

Laura Grant had encouraged her only son. She'd always been supportive, but she would never stand up for Dick against her husband. A spoiled, often selfish woman, Laura rarely went out of her way to defend anyone else.

Dick shook hands as his father descended on him, leaving a wake of interns and nurses behind him. "How was the vacation?"

"Truly a grand tour. Absolutely grand!" The deep voice rolled like a wave.

"You look good, Dad," Dick said, noting how the summer heat had tanned his father's florid skin a coppery red. He tried to match his father's heartiness, but it sounded as out of character as it felt.

"Feel good, a little heavier, I admit." He slapped his ample paunch in evidence. "Speaking of gaining weight, your mother just had me paged. She's a veritable apostle. She couldn't wait to spread the good word. She told me to be sure to congratulate you, so I suppose I'd better. Your mother's a little woman, but she packs a mighty mean wallop." Chuckling deeply, he slapped his son resoundingly on the back.

Pretending that he was under his wife's thumb, when the exact opposite was true, was one of his father's little games that Dick detested most. Although always said with a laugh, it nonetheless left a disturbing aftertaste in the mouth, as if he were demeaning his wife. Dick tried to overlook it this time. He knew that where his father was concerned, he was usually guilty of overreacting.

"I called this morning. I was hoping to get you before you left so I could tell you both myself. Mother promised not to breathe a word, but you know Mother." Dick felt compelled to apologize to his father.

"No need to explain anything. Your mother couldn't keep a secret for five minutes if her life depended on it. You didn't waste any time, Junior, did you?" He poked Dick in the ribs with the clipboard he was carrying.

Dick winced. He hated being called Junior. He'd been Junior all his life, in every sense of the word. And even if he became the greatest doctor since Hippocrates, that's all he'd ever be to his father.

"But then you always do get right down to business," his father was booming on. "Too bad. I was hoping you'd have enough sense to hold off for a while. That way, if you wanted to, you could always get out of the whole messy affair once you got the girl out of your system. A baby complicates matters, though."

Dick's father had never liked Kathy. When she was dating Dick in high school, he had always referred to her as "that little snip." And since she'd been back in Springfield, he liked her even less.

"The affair you are apparently referring to happens to be my marriage," Dick retorted stiffly. "And I don't want to get out of it, now or ever."

He forced himself to keep his voice low and controlled. If anyone should overhear their conversation, the entire staff of Cedars Hospital would be buzzing about it in a matter of minutes.

"No need to get all riled up about it, Junior. I was just speaking my mind—doing my duty as a father to his son. Not that I expect you to listen to me, you never do. Anyway, it looks like it's too late to take my advice, even if you had a mind to."

Dick preferred his father's open hostility to the genial contempt with which he was usually favored. If the baby was a boy, he told himself, he'd know exactly what not to do. He'd be a supportive, patient, loving father. As a grown man, Dick realized that his father's criticisms and ever-rising demands were his peculiar way of expressing his love. But for most of his young life, Dick hadn't believed it at all. And now it was too late to make any difference. The damage had been done.

"Of course, you can imagine how your mother feels about this blessed event. She's mortified just thinking of what her friends will say." Dr. Grant lowered his voice and confided in his best, most professional manner, "They gossiped enough about your instant wedding. Now you've given them the answer they suspected all along. It was a shotgun wedding."

Dick fought back the urge to use his fist to wipe the condescending smile off his father's face. But the man was his father, like it or not. Furthermore, Dick knew if he tried, he'd most certainly end up flat on his face.

"Mother always believes the worst," he grimaced, "and never hesitates to voice her opinion."

"It doesn't matter what she believes or what the truth is. It's how it *looks* that's important."

Dick didn't want to get into an argument with his father in the middle of the hospital, so he bit his lip and kept quiet. "Was there anything else you wanted to say to me, Dad?" he asked tersely.

"I think that about sums it up," Dr. Grant chuckled. "Call it a guarded prognosis, if you like."

"There's no point in arguing with the chief of staff, is there?" Dick smiled grimly and turned away.

He couldn't believe it! Why did he always let his father get under his skin? It was his father's first day back at the hospital, and already Dick felt tenser than he had in a month. He should never have joined the staff of Cedars. All through medical school, he swore to himself that he'd go to a hospital where he wasn't always being judged as his father's son. But in the end, he'd caved in to his parents' pressures, agreeing to try Cedars for a year. It was one of the few times he'd taken their advice, and he'd regretted it ever since.

One year had led to two, then three, and now he was a married man with a wife and soon a baby to think of. For the first time since Kathy had broken the news to him, Dick felt caught in a trap.

Chapter Five

Mother Love

As Bert made her way down the street to keep her appointment, she marveled at how quickly the last months had passed. The leaves were already beginning to turn red-orange at the edges, and Mikey had returned to school over two weeks ago. Mikey. He seemed happy enough to be back at school, but Bert could never be sure. She was reluctant to question him closely for fear of driving him farther away from her.

And then the letter had arrived. Why would the school principal want to see Bert? And so early in the school year? His summons was folded securely in Bert's wallet as she strode purposefully toward the school. She hadn't been able to bring herself to show the letter to Bill. He was upset enough about Mikey as it was, without having *this* to worry about, too. But could Bert handle it on her own? If only she could get through to Mikey and somehow find the key to unlock his heart.

Papa Bauer cautioned patience, and he understood the boy better than any of them. Sometimes Bert wondered how she'd ever survive without Papa. No matter how shattering the crisis, he always seemed to know the best thing to do. Papa had offered to accompany her to the school, but Bert had reluctantly declined the offer, feeling it would somehow be disloyal to Bill. If he ever found out that she'd gone to Papa instead of him, he'd feel totally alienated, as if she, too, were trying to cut him off from Mikey.

Bill was still determined to take a second job. The night watchman position had fallen through because of his background. Alcoholics were poor risks as security guards, he'd been told. Though discouraged, he hadn't given up the idea. Now, he was trying to land a position as a part-time insurance salesman, figuring he could make his calls in the evening when most prospective clients would be home anyway.

"Mrs. Bauer."

Bert jumped at the sound of her name and looked up from her seat outside the principal's office.

"Mr. Bigelow will see you now." The secretary was smiling sympathetically. "Straight ahead, and it's the first door on your left. And Mrs. Bauer, good luck."

"Thank you," Bert replied quickly, anxious to be away. Everyone in the office, she realized with a rush of righteous anger, must know that she had a problem son. Mikey was only a young boy, and already he'd been labeled. If they'd suffered the trauma he had, they'd have problems, too, she thought indignantly. Breathing fire, Bert marched down the hall, prepared to do battle, if need be, for her son.

"Thank you for coming so promptly, Mrs. Bauer." The principal pressed her hand between both of his as if he were offering his condolences and motioned for her to sit down. "I'm most anxious to hear your views on this latest, most distressing episode with Michael."

Mr. Lawrence Bigelow was a trim, energetic man with a crown of neatly cropped snow-white hair and a smooth, slightly florid, complexion. A pair of black-rimmed glasses rested on the desk in front of him. Beneath his cool, unruffled manner and his mellifluous, maddeningly reasonable voice, he ruled his school with an iron hand, brooking no dissent and stressing the old-fashioned virtues of discipline and order. He wasn't the kind of man to melt at a mother's tears.

Bert leaned forward in her chair and studied him intently. "What exactly has Mikey done, Mr. Bigelow?"

"You mean he hasn't told you or your husband?"

"I'm afraid he hasn't said a word about any . . . any episode, as you call it, to either of us—or to his grandfather, although they are very close."

The principal shook his head. "I warned him in the strongest possible terms to discuss this matter with you both, before we proceed with any disciplinary action."

He rolled an unsharpened pencil between his fingers. "Mrs. Bauer, does your son have a history of stealing or shoplifting, anything at all of that nature?"

"If you're asking me if Mikey has a criminal record," Bert bristled, "the answer is no. And furthermore, Mr. Bigelow, I consider that a most offensive question."

"I don't want to upset you, Mrs. Bauer," he smiled thinly, "but we are talking about a very serious matter here today. A child's wallet was stolen from his locker yesterday. After an extensive search of the school, in which, I assure you, no student or teacher was above suspicion, the wallet was found in your son's jacket pocket."

The principal's words knocked the wind out of Bert. She felt exactly as if she'd been punched in the stomach. "Are you sure it was Mikey, and not some other child?" she managed to stammer.

Mr. Bigelow was shaking his head back and forth, without a shadow of a doubt. "Michael had the boy's wallet in his pocket. I removed it myself."

"He might have found it. Just picked it up and put it in his pocket. The other boy might have lost it."

The principal's head continued to shake, until Bert had to fight the urge to hold it still. "I wish I could tell you that you're right, Mrs. Bauer. But Michael didn't deny the charge when I confronted him with the evidence. In fact, he refused to say a word about the incident, although I went to great pains to stress its seriousness.

"It really came as no surprise to any of us. Your son is a problem child, Mrs. Bauer. I don't use this term lightly, especially to a parent. But there is no other way to describe Michael's behavior. He has a history of insolence and sullenness in the classroom. But this latest behavior is much more serious than anything in his past record. The other boy's parents have very kindly declined to press charges, so naturally the school will respect their wishes. Under the circumstances, though, I feel that I have no choice except to expel Michael. I don't like to do this, especially with a child as young as your son, but I don't see that I have any choice."

Bert's hands were clasped so tightly together that her fingernails dug into her skin. She couldn't let herself break down and cry. What had happened to her wonderful baby? Where had Mikey gone? Somehow, she should have protected him more when their life was dissolving. Maybe she should have stayed at home and battled it out with Bill, instead of running away from their problems. But it was too late for regrets; she had to concentrate on helping Mikey now.

Bert tried frantically to think what she could say to help her son. She knew he wasn't a thief. If he had taken the wallet, it wasn't from anything evil in him. He must have been compelled by some desperate streak of rebellion, or perhaps he was just crying for help.

"Mikey is a very disturbed little boy, Mr. Bigelow, I know that," she began slowly. "But I don't think that kicking him out of school at this point is the answer to his problems. I'm not trying to minimize the incident, but more than anything now, Mikey needs security and support."

"I'd like to help you, Mrs. Bauer," the principal replied smoothly, "but I don't see how we can allow Michael to continue at this school. We have certain rules. . . . You understand."

"I understand that we're talking about a troubled boy crying for help, who needs patience now, not punishment or more pressure." Though shaky, Bert's voice rang with the passion in her heart.

"Mikey is going through a very difficult period in his life," she explained as calmly as she could, "and the adjustment is terribly painful for him. As your records will show, he had two sudden and emotionally wrenching moves last year. He left school in the middle of the year to move to Arizona and then returned before the term was over. I know he's happy to be back in Springfield. Still, the abrupt changes in his life affected him deeply. For Mikey's sake, I wish you could find a way to give him another chance. I appreciate the difficulty of your position, but making an example of the boy is not the way to help anyone."

Nothing about Mr. Bigelow changed a hair. Not the expression on his face, nor the even tenor of his voice. "We can't allow behavior of this criminal nature to go unpunished. It would set a most dangerous precedent for the entire school. I assure you that I sympathize with your position, Mrs. Bauer, but—"

"I'm not asking for your sympathy," Bert cried out. "I'm begging you to give my son a second chance. Please. He must be helped before it's too late!"

The senior Dr. Grant's large, porticoed white house sat on the crest of a hill. A pair of painted flamingos perched on the wide, manicured lawn that rolled down from the house to a crescent-shaped gravel drive, now filled with cars. Wedging her new forest-green Ford into the last available space, Meta turned to Bert with a wicked smirk. "Do you think Laura Grant was out on the grass this morning on her hands and knees picking up every autumn leaf that dared fall?"

"I hadn't thought about it, but now that you mention it, there isn't a single leaf on that entire lawn." Bert sounded astonished. She'd been so preoccupied since her interview with Mikey's principal that she hadn't seen a thing, even though she'd been staring out the car window. Now, looking around the Grants' immaculate yard, she couldn't hide her amazement. "How do you think they do it? The only sign of disorder I see anywhere is that pile of burned leaves over by the garage."

"Well, that is a surprise," Meta laughed. "Maybe Laura is made out of more than curlers and girdles after all."

For once Bert was thankful for her sister-in-law's caustic wit. It was impossible to brood over her family problems with Meta at her elbow making irreverent comments. Giggling like naughty schoolgirls, the two women started up the slate walk. Each one was carrying a present wrapped in pastel paper that showed pictures of teddy bears and rattles.

"How sweet! The other side of the family—and you came together," Laura Grant gushed at them from the door.

"United we stand," Meta quipped.

Laughing gaily, Laura ushered her newly arrived guests into the living room. The long, dark parlor was decorated to impress with its opulence. Heavy brocade draperies created a formal, and distinctly rich, tone. Elaborate needlepointing covered the sofas and several of the chairs. The mahogany tables gleamed with polish. Glancing around curiously, Meta was sure that Laura had decorated it herself, probably with the aid of a much-harassed interior designer.

Sprays of gold and russet chrysanthemums arranged with branches of autumn leaves stood sentinel at either side of the mantelpiece. On top, a delicate Dresden shepherdess held a lamb on her shoulder. A smaller arrangement of autumnal flowers and foliage squatted in a heavy cut-glass bowl on the coffee table. At the far end of the room, a baby grand piano stood open, as if waiting for the concert to begin.

Meta wouldn't have been the least bit surprised if Laura Grant swept over and launched into a Mozart sonata. Laura considered herself the most cultured person in Springfield and not only a patron of the arts, but also a person of considerable talent. Why, the whole town knew that as a mere slip of a girl, Laura

Ashley Grant had studied with the world-renowned Madame Novanshky in New York. What was less commonly realized was that she'd lasted only a month.

"Your house is stunning, Laura," Bert enthused. Her own home was such a hodgepodge. Except to replace something that was worn beyond repair, it was difficult to make any changes without somehow seeming disloyal to Mama Bauer. Much as she loved Papa, Bert wished sometimes that she had a house of her own. She knew exactly how she'd decorate each room. "Did you decorate it yourself?"

"Well, thank you, Bert dear." Laura accepted the compliment with modest grace. "Actually though, I did have a consultant. But he was more trouble than he was worth, since I knew just what I wanted. I always do—and Dick Sr. says I always get it, one way or another." The trilling laugh with which she delivered her little speech softened the determination in her words.

"You're much too modest, Laura," Meta cut in sarcastically.

Meta didn't dislike Kathy's new mother-in-law, just her presistent game-playing. She sometimes wondered how Richard and Laura Grant had ever produced a son like Dick, a decent, dedicated young man, utterly lacking in pretensions. Meta bit her tongue before she said something outrageous. The few times she'd met Laura Grant she'd been tempted to do or say something shocking, just to see if the woman would turn a hair. She was so perfect, so contained, so thoroughly playing her part that it was maddening. Meta suspected that Laura Ashley had never really existed until she became Mrs. Richard Grant, Sr., wife of the chief of surgery at Cedars Hospital. Now her days were filled with every charitable work in town, from supporting the floundering arts in Springfield to organizing a women's auxiliary at the hospital.

"Where's the girl of the hour?" Meta inquired with as much sweetness as she could muster.

"Right over there." Laura pointed to a cluster of women at the far end of the room. "She's been waiting anxiously for your arrival—even though you're not really family, are you?" she added cuttingly. "Still, I knew Kathy would want me to invite you."

Although Laura had managed to round up a couple of Kathy's high school friends, all of whom were married and with children, most of the women were her own friends. Laura fluttered among them, playing the role of the concerned grandmother-to-be to the hilt. She couldn't stop people from talking altogether, but she could work her hardest to make them bite their malicious tongues. Her husband told her that she was wasting her time and his money, but she had to try and quiet the gossips anyway. How could she be expected to show her face in town if everyone believed it was a shotgun wedding?

"Kathy, dear, I have two more *large* surprises for you." Laura stressed the word large, leaving no doubt that she was referring to the size of her guests. She felt diminished and slightly intimidated beside Meta's tall, commanding figure.

"I'm so glad you could come, Bert," Kathy admitted in a whisper as Bert bent down to kiss her. She was ensconced in an armchair, looking distinctly uncomfortable, like a prisoner who had just been denied her final appeal.

"I was thrilled to be invited." Bert smiled warmly at the girl. Although she scarcely knew Kathy, she was fond of Joe Roberts and she was sure that being Laura Grant's daughter-in-law wasn't going to be easy.

"You too, Meta," Kathy acknowledged, and for once she really meant it. She was glad to have her stepmother beside her.

"Buck up," Meta winked conspiratorially. "Once you've conquered this group, you've got nothing to fear."

"Here's hoping," she smiled grimly.

Even though she knew her mother-in-law didn't like her any better than Dr. Grant did, Kathy had no choice but to suffer through this baby shower. Laura had insisted on giving it, and it would be dangerous for Kathy to antagonize her in-laws any further. Laura Grant possessed a subtle but nonetheless powerful influence over her only son. While he sometimes resented her meddling, Dick loved her and listened to her advice.

Before Kathy and Meta had a chance to say anything more, Laura was clapping her hands together as if she were calling one of her volunteer committees to order. "Form a circle, now, girls, so we can open all these lovely presents," she called brightly.

Feigning a happiness she didn't feel, Kathy

tackled the stack of gifts. Cuddly stuffed animals, sweaters, nightgowns, and bonnets—all chosen in carefully neutral colors so they would be suitable for a girl or boy—spilled over her feet. Kathy oohed and aahed over each present, thanking every guest warmly. She was handling herself graciously, Meta thought. Joe would be proud.

When Kathy had finished opening the last box, Laura took the floor and with a carefully rehearsed speech delivered for the edification of her guests, presented her daughter-in-law with an intricate, handmade carriage robe.

Meta and Bert exchanged surprised glances. Laura must have been up all night for weeks making it in time for the baby shower. And no one could deny it was beautiful. Delicate tones of rose, cornflower blue, and white intermingled in the subtlest of patterns, and in the center of it all was a wreath of white blossoms, like baby's breath. The guests gasped admiringly, creating exactly the effect that Laura had planned.

Kathy thanked her awkwardly. She never knew exactly what to call her mother-in-law. Mrs. Grant sounded too formal, and Laura too familiar. But Kathy couldn't bring herself to say Mother Grant, although she knew that's what her mother-in-law expected. Her own mother had died when she was nine. She'd never called anyone Mother since and she wasn't about to begin now—especially with Dick's mother, who didn't even like her. As a result, she tried to avoid using a name at all costs.

Interrupting Kathy's thanks with a self-conscious laugh, Laura pecked her daughter-in-

law on the cheek and said loudly, "Father Grant
and I are so proud of you both. We simply can't
wait for the blessed event."

Before Kathy had time to reply, Laura was
signalling to the maid to pass the refreshments.

Meta chose a fingertip sandwich from a silver
tray and bit into a half-moon of watercress. Out
of the corner of her eye she could see Laura
making a beeline for her. Grandmothers in
crime, Meta thought sardonically. She looked
around quickly for an avenue of escape, but
Laura grasped her arm, trapping her with an
insistent, manicured hand.

"I do apologize, Meta. I haven't had a chance
to say more than two words to you since you
arrived, and we have so much to talk about—
becoming grandmothers together." She spoke
loudly for the benefit of the other women, all
the while subtly drawing Meta apart until she
had distanced them enough from the party not
to risk being overheard.

"I don't want any of those busybodies
listening in," she confided. "They all have
wagging tongues, though I can't deny that the
children have given them plenty to gossip
about." Laura sighed deeply as if the cares of
the world weighed on her slight shoulders. "It's
so distressing. I don't know how you and Joe
are handling the delicate matter, but Dr. Grant
and I are trying to keep our heads high, in spite
of the shame."

Meta stared at her with undisguised contempt.
"Since when is there anything shameful in a
husband and wife having a baby?"

"But so soon and after such a hasty wedding? It's downright indecent," Laura protested. "I won't deny I've been counting the months, everyone in Springfield has. It was the first question I asked Dick when he called at the crack of dawn with his awful news. I just knew it would be the question everyone in town would be asking. You can imagine what he said."

"Knowing Dick, the absolute truth," Meta retorted.

"Of course I don't blame Dick for a moment," Laura said pointedly. If there had been any hanky-panky going on, she knew who was responsible. Laura had never liked Kathy, and never made any effort to disguise the fact. Kathy was pretty enough, but she was a smart aleck, not at all the pliable, unassuming type of girl Laura had wanted for her son. "I'm praying the baby will be late."

Chapter Six

A Christmas Surprise

Kathy looked at the boxes and bags piled up on the bed and resisted the urge to push them on the floor and lie down. She was exhausted after shopping all afternoon with her mother-in-law for a layette. The throngs of Christmas shoppers and the bone-chilling cold had been too much for her, not to mention the company. Still, they had gotten pretty things for the baby.

Kicking off her shoes, she eased herself down on the edge of the bed and began emptying the shopping bags. It would only take a minute, and then she'd be done. Kathy knew she shouldn't complain. Her pregnancy was going smoothly. Dick was still as excited as he'd been the first day she told him; her father was proud, and in a few days it would be Christmas.

Kathy should be deliriously happy. But she wasn't. In fact, she was thoroughly miserable. And the closer she came to her due date, the more miserable she grew. She hated the ungainly, awkward way she moved with her cumbersome, swollen body. No matter what she put on, she looked like a circus freak. She'd never realized there were so many pencil-thin, supremely chic women in the world before. Absolutely no one looked overweight, except her.

Kathy never looked at herself in the mirror anymore. But shopping today she couldn't avoid it. There were mirrors everywhere, just waiting to shock her with her grotesque reflection, waddling behind her stylish mother-in-law.

Most of all, Kathy hated the lie she was living. She wanted to weep every day. For she'd slowly begun to realize that in the six months since their wedding, she'd truly fallen in love with her husband. His tenderness, decency, and strong, abiding love for her had won her heart. She found herself missing him whenever he was away and needing him more than she ever thought she would. How could she have deceived him?

But if Kathy confessed her guilty secrets now, Dick would never believe her. He was so concerned about her, so full of plans for his son or daughter. She wished she'd been honest with him at the beginning. If only she'd trusted his love enough to confide in him. . . .

Kathy clutched her stomach as a stab of pain shot through to her back. The baby had been in a good position, now she felt it somersaulting inside her. Gritting her teeth, she picked up a stack of bellybands and diapers and arranged them neatly in a bureau drawer. The nightgowns, sweaters, and caps went in the drawer below, the crib sheets and pads in the bottom drawer. All that remained to be put away were the receiving blankets.

Kathy picked up a pile of them and pressed them against her cheek. The soft flannel felt comforting. All the clothes she'd bought were so tiny and doll-like, she couldn't imagine a real-life baby fitting into them. Although she was still a little shaky, she dragged a stepladder over to the closet and climbed up to put the blankets on the shelf. The neat pastel stack looked like the colors on an Impressionist painter's palette. She leaned back a fraction to admire them better. Just as she did, her body cramped with pain.

Stifling a cry, Kathy let go of the stepladder and instinctively grasped her stomach, as if to guard the baby against the pain that was knifing through her. Her mouth went as dry as tissue paper. A line of sweat beaded her forehead. She felt herself catapulting backwards.

"Dick! Dick!" Kathy cried in anguish.

She tried to grasp the stepladder again, but flailed instead at the empty air.

When Kathy opened her eyes again, the room was spinning in dizzying motion. The silence was deafening. Her first sensation was pain—torturous, relentless, white pain. The overturned stepladder was angled against her swollen belly. She tried to push it off, but the effort intensified the pain. And now she was aware, too, of a dull ache in her right ankle. Kathy lay back on the floor and waited, praying the agony would pass. She wanted to scream and scream, but she forced herself to lie still and count. The pains were becoming even stronger and closer together. Tidal waves of them washed over her. A sudden gush of water drenched her. She was going to deliver her baby here—alone on the floor.

Kathy battled the deadly panic that was immobilizing her. She couldn't wait for Dick or Meta to come and get her. She couldn't wait for anything. The telephone was in the other room, far out of reach. She had to get to the hospital as fast as she could. Willing herself not to faint, she rolled over and pulled up her knees until she was crouching on all fours; then, half-dragging, half-crawling, she inched over to the bed. It took every ounce of strength she had left to pull herself up.

Kathy collapsed onto the bed. Tears streaked her already moist face. Her breath came in short, dry gasps. It's too soon . . . too soon, she kept repeating. But the pain didn't stop. Like the wildest surf, it rolled and crashed against her, each surge harder and stronger than the one before.

She tried to stand up, but her ankle buckled the moment she put her weight on it, and she caught hold of the bed post to keep herself from falling again.

The distance from the bedroom through the kitchen to the back door of their ground-floor apartment stretched ahead of her like a marathon course. Pushing back the hair that was sticking to her perspiring face, Kathy began to make her way around the room from bed to chair to bureau. She had to pause every two or three steps to catch her breath, but she finally made it to the door. Although her ankle was throbbing now, it was nothing compared to the other pain she felt. No one had prepared her for the agony of labor.

Just a few more yards, she kept telling herself. Reaching along the kitchen counter, she found her car keys and opened the back door. A gust of icy wind buffeted her. She staggered, shivering violently against the bitter onslaught. Her plaid maternity dress slapped at her knees. She hadn't thought to grab her coat, and she couldn't turn back now.

Leaning against the door frame to steady herself, she prayed that Dick would come home. Or a neighbor would go by—anyone who could help her. The distance to the car yawned like the Grand Canyon. She'd never make it—but she had to. She'd freeze to death or die in childbirth if she didn't. It might be better for all of them, she thought, if she and the baby did die. It would certainly make everything easier.

For a moment, Kathy indulged the dangerous thought, but fear forced her to reject it. What if she survived and only the baby died? A fresh wave of pain assaulted her, even worse than before. It was now or never. With her last remaining strength, she staggered forward and hurled herself in the direction of the car. It was parked only six feet from the door, but it might as well have been miles. She lunged for the handle to keep from fainting and yanked it open.

Breathless and panting, Kathy slumped on the seat. Her teeth chattered uncontrollably.

Her body trembled from the effort she had exerted and from the spiraling pain that gnashed at it. Still, she felt safe at last. Deliberately, she inserted the key in the ignition and started the engine. It turned over once, then died. She tried a second time, and a second time it died. Fighting back the urge to try again, Kathy forced herself to sit back and wait. She didn't want to flood the car. Finally, she pulled the choke out halfway and turned the ignition again. The motor purred. She revved it until it roared, then, slamming the clutch into gear, she shot out the driveway.

Kathy drove as though street signs and traffic lights didn't exist. Weaving wildly through the traffic, she sped without stopping until she reached the towering iron gates of Cedars Hospital. Somewhere in that mass of concrete and steel, Dick was waiting for her. She had to find him. Braking at the front entrance, she eased herself across the seat and pushed the door open.

"Dick, Dick," she moaned as she crumpled over and the pavement came up to meet her. A black shroud enveloped her, and she felt herself sinking inescapably into oblivion.

"I'm right here, darling. You're going to be fine now. It's almost over."

A cool hand caressed her forehead, but Kathy only closed her eyes tighter as a searing pain tore through her, so severe that she felt as if she were being ripped apart. Her body jackknifed. Muffled voices came to her from a long distance.

"Will you page Dr. Steadman? Have him

meet me in the delivery room right away."

"I'm sorry, Dr. Grant, Dr. Steadman left not more than ten minutes ago. He couldn't even have gotten home yet."

"Well try him for me anyway, please—and keep trying until you get him."

When the pain slackened, Kathy opened her eyes slowly. She was lying on a stretcher. A white sheet was drawn up to her waist. An IV needle was feeding into her arm. She could see Dick just a few steps away at the front desk talking on the telephone. Even though his back was toward her, Kathy felt safe at last. She didn't have to fight anymore. Dick would take care of everything. The agonizing pain was tapering into a dull stabbing. Her eyes closed again as if the lids were too heavy to hold open.

Kathy was already sleeping soundly when Dick came over and took her hand. Her pulse was returning to normal. The medication in the IV was taking effect. At least the physical pain would be over now, but it might be too late to save the baby. Grimly, he followed the stretcher into the elevator.

It took only seconds to reach the maternity floor, but to Dick it felt like hours—precious hours that could mean life or death to his unborn child. He rushed out of the elevator ahead of the stretcher and began galvanizing the nurses with his curt, tense orders.

"I've got an emergency here. Prepare the delivery room."

"What's the patient's name, Doctor?" the floor nurse asked.

"Kathy Grant," Dick choked. "She's my wife."

"I'm sorry, Dr. Grant," she gasped in surprise. "Will Dr. Steadman be on his way?"

Dick shook his head. "He can't get here in time."

"Then who—?"

"I'll deliver her myself."

"But you can't, Doctor. She's your wife. The hospital rules—" she began to protest.

"Damn the rules." He brushed by her and went into scrub. "This is an emergency!"

The floor nurse was at his heels in an instant. "I can't allow you to do this, Dr. Grant. I know my responsibilities."

"And I know mine," he ground through clenched teeth. "So don't try to stop me."

Kathy lay on the operating table, oblivious to everything—the rubber cone of ether over her nose, the cold steel stirrups that supported her feet, and the grim young doctor who attended her. There had been no time to prepare her for the delivery. The baby's head was already visible.

"Come on, darling," Dick urged, "one last big push and we'll be home free."

He tried to put his emotions aside, as he did with every other operation. But he couldn't. This wasn't a patient. This was his love—his life.

"Push, Kathy, push," he urged, even though he knew she couldn't hear him. Her body was cut off from her unconscious mind, responding as best it could to the new life struggling to be free of it. The steamy cavern that had been its home since conception, nurturing and sheltering it, had in the last few minutes become its prison. He held the forceps ready to ease the baby out as soon as there was enough to grasp.

"How's she doing?"

Dick looked up, startled and then relieved by the familiar voice. "It's touch and go," he answered grimly. "I think Kathy will be OK, but the baby. . . ." His voice trailed off. "What are you doing here anyway, Peggy?"

"I was just going off duty when I heard you'd brought Kathy in." Peggy Regan took in the situation with a quick, practiced eye. Although she was a floor supervisor now, she'd been the chief obstetrics nurse at Cedars for years.

"I didn't bring her in. She brought herself. She was already in heavy labor. God knows how she got herself here. She was bleeding badly." Dick's staccato sentences dropped like bullets into the silence of the operating room.

"Poor kid!" Peggy shook her head sympathetically and reached out to stroke Kathy's leg. It seemed only yesterday that she had been a mischievous little girl with coltlike legs and long blond pigtails. Peggy had come to love the motherless child—and her father, too. The Robertses were the only real family Peggy had ever known. For a while she'd hoped—even dared to dream—that she'd truly become a part of it. Then Joe met Meta Bauer.

Peggy shook loose her memories and turned to Dick with concern. Kathy wasn't just a patient to Peggy, either, but she had many more years experience behind her than Dick. She remembered the night he was born right here at Cedars. Dr. Grant had had champagne and cigars delivered to every floor to celebrate the birth of his first son, and the nurses had immediately nicknamed the infant "Baby Doc."

Peggy palpated Kathy's stomach. The baby was motionless. Every second now could mean the difference between life and death. The baby was premature, so it should slip right out. But the opening was so small. She couldn't let anything happen to Kathy or her baby.

"Have you cut her yet, Dick?" she asked gently.

He shook his head. "No." The word emitted was more a desperate cry of refusal than a reply.

"You know you have to. Right now. You don't have a second to spare." She pressed him, knowing that often the toughest decision is really the kindest.

"I can't," he answered starkly.

"You're a doctor, and right now she's your patient first, and your wife second. How can you refuse her the same professional treatment you would give to any other woman?"

Tears sprang to Dick's eyes. "I can't put a knife into Kathy," he cried.

"You can. And you will, if you love her enough. If you don't, you're going to lose her baby. *You* will. No one else." Peggy hated the brutal frankness of her words, but she knew it was the only hope.

"Hang on, honey," she murmured as Dick took the scalpel she held out to him. "We're coming to get you."

With a sharp intake of breath, Dick angled the blade against his wife's skin and drew it down in a quick, clean incision. Tears rolled down his cheeks, dampening his surgical mask, as he withdrew the knife.

"It's coming," Peggy cried tensely.

Dick reached up and caught the baby as it slithered free at last. "You slap her, Peg," he murmured hoarsely. "I've done enough violence to my family for one day, or one lifetime."

"You didn't do much of anything, except save this little tyke's life. Kathy will hardly feel a twinge tomorrow." Peggy spanked the baby soundly.

For an infinite fraction of a second, they waited, drowning in the silence. Then the baby screamed, filling its little lungs with the first breath of life. Laughing and crying, Dick cradled the slippery body and kissed her downy head.

"I was waiting for a special Valentine, instead I got a Christmas miracle," he cooed to the still bawling baby. "We were going to call you Robin, if you were a girl, because we thought you'd be the first sign that Spring was coming soon. I guess we'll still call you Robin, if your mama agrees, because that's how I've been thinking of you every day. Robin Katherine Grant, meet the greatest nurse in the world." Beaming proudly, he held his daughter out to Peggy.

"Pleased to meet you, I'm sure," she laughed. "and you don't look any the worse for wear."

Peggy had had the incubator ready, expecting a tiny, premature infant. But Robin Katherine Grant, though fragile, weighed a solid five and a half pounds. While Dick took care of Kathy, she bathed the baby in warm water, diapered her and wrapped her tightly in a soft, white blanket.

With all the love and pride of the new father he naively believed he was, Dick took the baby and laid her in her mother's arms. Instinctively, the infant nuzzled into the warmth of her mother's breast.

Kathy's eyes opened slowly. She blinked several times to accustom them to the glaring light. Her body felt different, lighter somehow. She looked around in confusion at the strange, frighteningly sterile room. Where was she? What had happened? The baby. . . . She'd lost the baby. Panic gripped her. A stranger swathed in an ugly green cap and gown was standing over her, watching her. And he was smiling. The most glorious smile Kathy had ever seen wreathed his face.

"It's a girl," he murmured, bending down to brush her forehead with a kiss. "A beautiful baby girl, just like her mama."

"Dick," Kathy whispered weakly.

She reached out to him, and as she did, she became aware for the first time of the fragile bundle on her chest. It was so light, it felt weightless. Her fingers grazed the baby's petal-soft skin.

"Robin Katherine Grant," Dick murmured, "meet your wonderful mother."

Kathy gazed down at her new daughter with soft, liquid eyes, and sat up with a jerk. Bob Lang's insouciant, all-American face was looking up at her. With a violent shudder, she pushed the baby away.

"No! No! I can't bear to see her. Take her away," she sobbed hysterically to her stunned husband. "I don't want her. I never wanted her."

Chapter Seven

An Unwelcome Baby

"Merry Christmas, darling!"

Kathy turned over on her side and curled up, hunching her knees against her chest in her favorite sleeping position. It registered, somewhere at the outskirts of her mind, that she hadn't been able to lie like that in months.

"Not Christmas for a whole week yet," she mumbled sleepily, snuggling lower under the blankets until all that was left exposed was the tip of her upturned nose.

Dick looked from his drowsy wife back to the tiny bundle he cradled lovingly in his arms. Baby Robin opened her eyes. They were a bright, sparkling, summer's day blue. Although he thought that newborn babies weren't supposed to be able to focus, Dick was sure that Robin was looking directly up at him.

"You know your daddy already, don't you, my beauty? Of course you do," he cooed, tickling her under the chin. "And now you're going to get to know your beautiful mama.''

Dick thought that he could be perfectly happy for the rest of his life just holding his daughter. And he was sure that now that her frightening labor was over, Kathy would love their baby as much as he did. Though still shocked by her rejection in the delivery room, he tried to dismiss it. It was an irrational reaction to the agony she'd just endured, or perhaps a protective instinct triggered by her unspoken fears that the infant, born so prematurely, might not survive. He couldn't wait to see Kathy's face when she held their baby for the first time.

"Darling, wake up," he urged tenderly. "I have a Christmas surprise for you."

Kathy flung herself over on her back again and stretched languidly.

"I wanted to get something very special for you, and now I can't get you anything at all," she complained sulkily.

"Nothing?" Dick laughed. "You've just given me the most wonderful Christmas present any man could ever have. Open your eyes, darling, and see for yourself. We're the luckiest two people in the world." Dick balanced Robin in the wide palm of his hand and held her up for her mother to admire. "What do you think, Kathy?" he beamed. "We did a pretty good job if you ask me."

Kathy's face hardened at the unwelcome sight. Why couldn't the squirming, red-faced creature have died, she thought bitterly. Then she and Dick could start all over again and make a lovely new baby—one that was really their own. The love on Dick's face was so clear as he held the baby, Kathy wanted to weep.

As if she could see and understand the expression on her mother's face, Robin began to cry. Bewildered, Dick held the baby up against his shoulder to comfort her.

"See," he tried not to let his voice betray his concern, "Robin wants her mama. Just hold her a minute and soothe her, darling. She's probably ready to nurse anyway," he coaxed.

Kathy flung an arm across her eyes to shut out the picture she couldn't bear to face. How could she ever have believed that such a cruel deception would work?

"No," she said dully. "Take her away, please, Dick, and don't bring her back in here. Can't you understand? I don't want to see her, or hold her, or do anything with her."

Instinctively, Dick held his daughter tighter. "You're exhausted and upset. You don't know what you're saying." His words, which echoed in the cold, impersonal room, were a desperate plea. But Kathy was saved from answering by an eager tap at the door.

"Congratulations!" Joe Roberts called, poking his head in the door. "Is the proudest grandfather—and father—in the whole United States permitted to see his two best girls?"

Bearing a fragrant old-fashioned bouquet of pink sweetheart roses and baby's breath framed by a lace doily and tied with pink streamers, he marched in as proud as could be.

"Daddy!" Kathy cried in astonishment. "You're walking. I can't believe it!" She sat bolt upright in bed and, for the first time in forty-eight hours, smiled.

"I told you I'd be out of that darn chair in time to take my grandchild out in her carriage," he said, squeezing Dick's shoulder and then folding Kathy in his arms. "If she's one tenth as pretty as you were when you were born, she'll be a beauty."

Father and daughter looked at each other for a long moment, alone together through a mist of tears.

"Oh, Daddy." Kathy threw her arms around his neck. "I'm so glad you're here. It's so awful . . . I don't want you to even think about the baby."

Joe tried to shrug off her unexpected words. "Not think about my first granddaughter? Why, that's all I've been thinking about for months— the baby and you, of course, Kathy. No one will ever replace you in my heart. But little Robin. . . ."

"Forget she was ever born," Kathy interrupted tearfully. "We're going to give her up for adoption. It's the only way. You'll see." She sobbed her heart out on her father's shoulder.

Speechless, Joe just held her and let her cry. He sought some explanation in his son-in-law's face for Kathy's disturbing behavior. But Dick could only shake his head in answer to the questioning look. At the word adoption, he'd gasped. But he was so stunned that when he opened his mouth to protest, no sound came out. Uncomprehending and utterly helpless, the two men waited for Kathy's sobs to quiet. The beautiful bouquet lay forgotten on the bed.

Meta had been hovering just inside the door,

all of her attention centered on Joe. She was ready to rush to his side if he falthered. Though short, the distance from the door to Kathy's bed was like Mt. Everest for him. He hadn't walked a single step without a cane or an arm to support him before this. In fact, his wheelchair stood waiting right outside the door where he'd abandoned it for the first time. Kathy's shocking words, though, were like receiving a jolt of electricity.

In contrast to Joe and Dick, Meta felt neither pity nor disbelief. Only anger—a deep, white, uncontrollable rage at the spoiled, selfish girl. Kathy had wrecked her father's life. Now she was threatening to do the same to her husband and newborn baby. Throughout Kathy's pregnancy, an unspoken truce had prevailed between the two strong-willed women. As far as Meta was concerned, it was over.

"Shut up, Kathy, and don't you ever dare breathe the word adoption again," she hissed, as if the very word were full of venom. "You don't know what you're talking about. But I do. Dear God, do I ever. You think you've suffered?" she scoffed. "It's nothing to the pain of having to deny your own innocent baby. I know what it's like to have a heart overflowing with love and not be free to express it. I know what it's like to watch my own baby raise his arms to another woman and call her Mama."

She advanced on Kathy breathing fire. "You'll probably always be a spoiled brat, but now you're a mother, too—and you damn well better cut out this nonsense and begin acting like one."

Kathy's sobs had stopped abruptly and she'd drawn away from her father as if answering some primitive urge to confront her enemy with all her strength. From the first, she'd known that Meta would be the most formidable obstacle to resolving this unwanted pregnancy. She was prepared for the physical blow that she was sure was going to follow the verbal attack. And she would answer it with tooth and nail. The time to have it out with Meta was long overdue. This woman who had barged into her father's life was responsible for everything, Kathy thought bitterly. If Meta had never seduced her father, she would have stayed in Springfield, married Dick, and had *his* baby— instead of another man's.

"Please, Meta." Joe tried to squelch the storm, reaching out a peacekeeping hand to his wife and daughter.

Kathy drew back, coiled to strike as soon as she was attacked. But Meta replied angrily.

"No, Joe. Not this time. I've watched from the sidelines and held my tongue long enough. But not anymore, not when this helpless baby's happiness is at stake."

Before any of them knew what she was doing, Meta swooped down like an eagle and plucked the baby out of Dick's arms.

"Where are you taking her?" he gasped. But before the question was even finished, the answer was clear.

With one stride of her long, slender legs, Meta reached the bed and deposited baby Robin in her mother's arms. For an instant, Kathy appeared so surprised that it looked as if

94

she might drop the infant. But Robin's tiny fingers reached out and grasped her mother's. Looking down at the defenseless child in her arms, Kathy felt a sudden rush of love and protectiveness unlike anything she'd ever known before. How could she have considered abandoning her baby? She clutched Robin to her breast and, weeping helplessly, turned her face to the wall, too ashamed to face her husband or her father again.

With tears in her own eyes, a trembling Meta motioned to Dick and Joe, and the three of them tiptoed out of the hospital room, leaving mother and child alone together.

Hours later, when Peggy Regan stopped by to visit, Kathy was sleeping soundly, still clutching the infant protectively. Gently, Peggy eased the tiny burden from her mother's arms and carried it back to the nursery to be changed and fed.

The nursery was crowded. All but three of the small white cribs were filled with newborn babies, some squirming, some squalling, and some sleeping peacefully through the turmoil. The neonatal nurse in attendance was busy holding up babies for excited relatives to ogle at through the broad picture window, so Peggy began to change Robin herself. She was just about to wrap her up in a fresh dry blanket when she glanced around to find Janet Johnson at her elbow.

"You're pretty far from your bailiwick, aren't you, Janet?" Peggy asked, assessing the younger nurse curiously.

"I'm on my supper break," Janet replied

defensively. She didn't want her supervisor to think she was shirking her duties. "I thought I'd just peek in and get a look at the Grants' baby. This is the one, isn't it?"

"Robin Grant, and she certainly is pretty, isn't she?" Peggy smiled as if she were the grandmother herself. "Poor Kathy had a hard time of it, but no damage to mother or baby, thank goodness."

"Is it true that Dick—I mean Dr. Grant—delivered her himself?" Janet was still staring intently at the baby as if she were memorizing every inch of her.

"My, my, but the grapevine must have been busy around here," Peggy frowned. "But yes, since you're all going to gossip about it anyway, he did—and a fine, courageous job he did, I might add."

"What's the old man going to say when the case comes up before the hospital board? You know the rules at Cedars—"

"Not a single thing," Peggy interrupted. "No one can, because Dick Grant did the only thing he could under the circumstances. There was no one else available at the time to deliver this little bundle of love." Peggy planted a decisive kiss on Robin's cheek as she wrapped the blanket under the baby. Something about Janet's tone was annoying her unreasonably. She wished the other nurse would go back to her own floor and let her feed Robin in peace. But Janet seemed reluctant to leave. There was something on her mind, something about the baby.

Like everyone at Cedars, Peggy knew that

Janet had been dating Dick Grant until Kathy came back to town. Probably the girl was still hurt from being so abruptly thrown over, maybe even aching that Robin wasn't her own little girl. Peggy could sympathize with the feeling. How many times she'd wished that Kathy were her daughter—or at least her stepdaughter.

"Would you like to hold Robin while I warm up a bottle?" she asked kindly. Janet seemed to hesitate, then she took the baby. Peggy hurriedly fixed the formula, unable to shake the uneasy feeling she had about leaving Kathy's baby with Janet. When she got back, Janet was exactly where Peggy had left her, as if she were rooted to the spot. She was staring intently at the infant she was bouncing lightly up and down in the open palms of her hands, as if mentally weighing and measuring her.

"I expected to find her in an incubator," Janet said thoughtfully when Peggy returned.

"Why's that?" Peggy asked tersely.

"Well, she's supposed to be a preemie, isn't she—although she certainly doesn't look like one to me. Of course, I'm no expert on babies," she added hastily.

"We had the incubator ready. But since she weighed over five pounds and appeared to be a fine, strong baby, we didn't think it was necessary," Peggy answered. For some reason she couldn't exactly pinpoint, she felt compelled to give Janet a full explanation.

Although Peggy had the bottle ready, Janet made no move to relinquish Robin. Instead, she continued weighing her, and the longer she held her the more calculating her expression became.

"Shouldn't you be getting back on duty?" Peggy prodded, anxious to feed Robin.

"Oh, I've still got a few minutes yet," Janet said, brushing the hint aside airily.

"Well, maybe you have, but Robin doesn't," Peggy replied firmly, retrieving the infant. Gently she took Robin's fist out of her mouth and inserted the nipple. The baby sucked gratefully under Janet's hawklike eye.

"Do preemies usually eat that much?" she asked with elaborate innocence. "Being an obstetrical nurse for as many years as you were, you must be an expert on these things," she added fawningly.

"Every baby is different." Peggy curved the baby closer in her arm, as if to protect her from the other nurse's unpleasant questions.

"Well, Peggy, just between the two of us, if this baby is premature, then so is every other kid in the nursery." Janet swept the other cribs with a glance. She arched a brow knowingly. "It may be a month early, but there's no way in the world that it's two or three months."

Peggy glared at Janet with icy eyes. "Exactly what is it that you're insinuating?" she demanded.

"Nothing," she said, with offended dignity. "I was just remembering what everyone in Springfield has been saying ever since Dick Grant's wedding."

"I presume that you mean Dick married Kathy Roberts because he got her pregnant?" Peggy tried to keep her voice calm. She knew what it was like to love and lose, and to know loneliness with painful intimacy. And so a part of her sympathized with Janet.

"Almost," she replied slowly, as if she were pondering the theory of relativity. "But the theory doesn't quite fit, does it?"

"What on earth are you talking about?" Peggy exploded.

"Nothing, except little Robin here doesn't look anything like Dick, do you think? And if she's only a month early—or maybe even just a week or two—then one can't help wondering. . . ."

"That's enough, Miss Johnson," Peggy snapped. Her lips were white and her naturally warm eyes had frosted over. "I won't listen to any more of your snide insinuations. Just because you lost out to a better woman, it doesn't give you any right to blacken the names of two fine families. If you know what's good for you, you'll get back to your floor immediately. And if so much as a whiff of your vile accusations gets back to me, I'll make it my personal business to see that you never work at Cedars Hospital again. Have I made myself clear, Miss Johnson?" Peggy demanded hotly.

A sly, knowing smile spread slowly over Janet's face. "That's not all you've made clear, Miss Regan."

Peggy turned her back abruptly. She didn't want the other nurse to see the fear reflected in her eyes. Although she hadn't put it together before, it all fit with sickening precision: the timing, the size of the baby, and, most damning of all, Kathy's unexpected reaction. In her heart, Peggy suspected that Janet was right. But she wasn't about to listen to any criticism of the Roberts' family.

Chapter Eight

Confirming Suspicions

Kathy sat up in bed, feeling stronger and more hopeless than she had anytime since the baby was born. She'd showered for the first time in the hospital and washed and brushed her hair until it shone like golden sunbeams. Although she wore the peach satin bed jacket she'd bought for her wedding trousseau, her spirits were so low the beautiful jacket felt more like a prison uniform. Looking outside the window, she watched the snow swirl down in dizzying eddies, which only added to her sense of confinement. Down the hall in the nursery, Robin slept contentedly, innocent of the torment her birth had created.

Kathy tried to blame everyone: Bob Lang, for taking advantage of her; Dick, for not making her confess before he married her; and most of all Meta, for interfering and ruining her last desperate plan. If she'd never held Robin or hugged her or felt her fragile fingers holding fast, she would have been able to give her up with little more than a twinge of regret. Now it was too late. Once awakened, a mother's love was infinite and without end.

Kathy tried to blame everyone, but it was a useless exercise. The finger of blame pointed in only one direction—at her own guilty heart. She felt trapped by her own deceit. Now that she'd accepted Robin, she could no longer bear to see Dick. He was so in love with the baby and with her, so utterly at the mercy of their affection, the truth would shatter him.

Absently, Kathy reached over and plucked a faded blossom from the massive white poinsettia that her in-laws had sent. It was the closest she'd come to them since Robin's birth. Although Dr. Grant stuck his head in every morning when he made rounds, Kathy had successfully managed to feign sleep each time. And, mercifully, Laura Grant was confined to bed with a virus. Something to be thankful for, at least, Kathy thought bleakly. She didn't think she'd ever be able to face their disapproving scrutiny again.

Shutting her eyes, she rested her head back on the pillow and wondered how different it would be if she'd had a mother of her own. Kathy had only the haziest memories of sparkling eyes and a wonderful smile, gleaned as much from old photographs as from her own childish recollections. She knew her father had loved her mother deeply—so much so that all the time she was growing up he had remained alone. No woman could replace her mother, although many tried, until Meta Bauer stormed into their lives.

Kathy opened her eyes to eradicate the image of her stepmother and found her true, second mother smiling down at her. With a little cry of surprise and relief, she opened her arms and fell against the soothing warmth of Peggy Regan's ample bosom as if she had found a sanctuary at last.

Peggy hugged her warmly, just as she had when she was a skinny little girl in need of mothering. "How do you feel, Kathy? You look as pretty as a picture, but then you always have in my eyes."

"I'm fat and hideous. I'll never be pretty again—or happy," Kathy blurted. "I've made such a mess of everything. How did you find me here, anyway?"

"It didn't require much detective work." Peggy chuckled with unshakable good humor. "The whole hospital is talking about young Dr. Grant's baby daughter."

Kathy groaned. "I can imagine what they're saying. I wish I'd never come back to Springfield. Daddy and Dick—and everybody—were doing just fine until then."

"And how about you?" Peggy probed gently.

"What do you mean?"

"Were you doing just fine, too?"

Kathy hesitated. "I grew up a lot while I was away, that's for sure."

"The way you've been behaving isn't exactly my idea of maturity," Peggy needled a little.

Kathy shook her head despondently. "You don't understand. Nobody does."

"Is that why you were so upset when you saw

the baby in the delivery room?"

"How do you know about that?" Kathy snapped.

"I was there," Peggy answered calmly. "I thought Dick could use a little help. Didn't he tell you?"

"I guess he hasn't had a chance. I haven't exactly been behaving the way a new mother is expected to, I suppose."

"Robin is a beauty." Peggy hesitated, undecided whether to say more or not. "We had the incubator ready," she began tentatively. "We always do for a preemie. But Robin didn't need it. Thank God she's a strong, healthy baby."

"She'll have to be to survive the mess I've already made of her life, and she's only two days old. She'll probably hate me for it. And if she doesn't, Dick will, and so will Daddy."

"Why don't you tell me about it, and let me help you?" Peggy urged softly.

"I can't," Kathy wailed.

Peggy stroked Kathy's hair soothingly with her large, comforting hand. Afternoon shadows began to gather in the corners of the quiet room. A nurse came to the door carrying Robin to her mother for a feeding, but Peggy motioned her away and returned to her rhythmic caressing. Gradually, she could feel Kathy's body relaxing and her breathing coming in smooth, even waves.

"Do you remember that time—you couldn't have been more than thirteen or fourteen— when you'd just begun to notice Dick? More than anything, you wanted him to carry your books home from school, and you were sure he wanted to. But he was just too shy to offer." Peggy smiled to herself at the innocent memory.

"Of course I remember," Kathy sniffled. "While I was trying to figure out how to approach him without actually coming right out and asking, that pushy Rosemary Halsey beat me to it. She walked right up to him bold as brass and dropped her books at his feet. I was so mad," Kathy admitted.

"I remember. Your father must have been working the graveyard shift that night, because I was sitting for you. You burst in the door and dissolved in tears, absolutely convinced that it was the end of your life. But even when they seem the most hopeless, things have a way of working themselves out. They will now, too," Peggy assured her.

"No. Not this time." Pulling away, Kathy threw herself down on the bed, burying her face in the pillow. Her muffled voice fell like a thunderclap in a field of snow. "You don't understand, Peggy. Robin isn't Dick's baby."

A strained silence enveloped the room. Peggy imagined that her own breathing was unnaturally loud. She scrambled for something to say to ease Kathy's guilt, but couldn't overcome her own shock. She didn't know why she was so stunned by the admission; she'd known Janet Johnson was right. Robin was too big to be a preemie. The only real surprise was that everyone who saw the baby wasn't buzzing about it.

"What are you trying to say, Kathy?" Peggy beld her breath and waited. She was afraid of what the answer would be, yet she had to help if she could.

Through the pillow Kathy's voice sounded flat and far away. "I was pregnant when I married Dick."

Peggy could understand running away, but getting herself pregnant! The reality refused to sink in. It was Kathy—little Kathy—they were talking about, with the swinging pigtails and infectious smile, the apple of her father's eye. How could she have done it to Joe? Peggy thought bleakly.

"Does Dick know yet?" she finally managed to murmur.

The heavy silence was answer enough.

Peggy touched Kathy's shoulder. "Do you want to talk about it?" she asked gently. "You know what you tell me will never go farther than this room. It sometimes helps to talk it out—to share your burden with someone who loves you."

"I don't know how to tell you, or where to begin," Kathy stammered.

"Try the beginning." Peggy tried to smile. "It's usually the best place to start."

Kathy glanced up quickly at Peggy, then averted her eyes again. Lying back on the pillow, her face turned to the wall, she began haltingly. "You know I went to New York when Daddy remarried."

Peggy nodded. "I heard something to that effect," she admitted ruefully.

"I guess everybody in Springfield knows about that," Kathy sighed "I didn't know anybody, or anything for that matter, although

I thought I knew it all. I must have been insufferable."

"You were always a forceful little girl," Peggy admitted, "but never insufferable."

"Anyway, I wanted to be a famous writer. All I had were my high school compositions and a couple of articles from the *Banner*, but I was sure that any publishing company would be thrilled to have me. I went to Lang & Co. At that time, it was probably the most prestigious publishing house in the country. I barged right into the president's office with every confidence in the world and presented my pathetic credentials." Kathy's words rushed on like a river after the winter thaw. The present faded as she talked until she felt almost as if she were back in New York in Bob's cluttered office. She pictured him again with startling clarity. She hadn't been fair to him, either. She'd used him just as cruelly as she was using Dick, but he hadn't let her get away with it without paying dearly. Knowingly or unknowingly, he'd exacted his price with Robin. And how he would have loved his daughter! The very thought was indescribably painful.

"He hired me on the spot. He told me later it was because I reminded him of himself years before. And he has controlled my life since that day." Kathy's voice sank so low that Peggy had to strain to catch her words.

"Who was this man?" she asked.

"Robert A. Lang, the last of a long line in a very distinguished Yankee family, Exeter and Harvard, an all-American, clean-cut man, casually elegant, always nonchalant—even when his heart was bleeding. His emotions were so well covered that when he did reveal them, it was a shock. I believe he loved me. In any event, he married me and gave me everything I wanted—and then some."

"You mean Robin?"

Kathy answered with a barely perceptible nod of her head. "He desperately wanted children and a wife who truly loved him. He never got either."

"Maybe there's still time."

"No." Kathy's voice quavered and she shook her head. "I was fond of him. I truly did care for him, and now I'm beginning to understand him. I never did while we were married. But I didn't love him. Anyway, none of that matters now. Bob Lang is dead."

"Is that why you came home?" Peggy's voice was little more than a whisper. In her mind, Kathy was young to be married, but to be a widow. . . .

"Bob inherited the family business," Kathy explained, as if now compelled to reveal every detail. "When he ran it into the ground, he sold out to a gang of mobsters to cover his failure. I stumbled across some discrepancies in the company books and confronted him with them driving home that night. When he finally confessed that the venerable firm of Lang & Co. had become a front for an organized crime syndicate, we had a terrible fight—our first, really. I was shocked and disgusted. All I could think of was Daddy. We argued bitterly. The worse things I said, the faster Bob drove. He didn't see a cab coming down the avenue until it

was too late. He swerved in time to save me—
and Robin." Kathy had to force each word out
now, but she still insisted on continuing. "I
guess I panicked. Anyway, I ran away."

"Are you sure your husband's dead?" Peggy
ventured.

"Yes," she answered flatly. "I watched him
crush like a can of tomatoes. Awful as it was,
that accident at least taught me what was
important in my life. I came home to make up
to Daddy—even to Meta, if I had to. I was going
to confess everything and start again. A new
life, a clean slate. I had no idea that Daddy had
become an old man while I was away. The shock
of having me home again was too much for him.
You know the rest, I suppose. He had a heart
attack when he saw me. We never had time to
talk, and by the time he was well again, I knew I
was pregnant. I didn't say anything, afraid
another shock would be fatal. Dick was
Daddy's doctor. He's never been able to hide
his feelings. I could see right away that he still
loved me—he'd never stopped loving me. . . ."
Kathy stopped. "Do I have to go on?"

"No," Peggy said slowly. "I know all too well
what it means to hold to a love you're sure will
never be answered."

For an instant the two women's eyes locked,
and Kathy saw reflected, as in a mirror, the pain
and sorrow that was in her heart. She took
Peggy's hand. "You love Daddy, don't you? I
never thought of it before, but I suppose you
did all those years you were mothering me."

"He's a wonderful man." Peggy smiled
wistfully. "We went out a few times when you

were very small, but he never loved me. He never loved any woman except your mother until he met Meta Bauer. I don't hold any grudge. He deserves every happiness."

"I wish I could be as generous as you. Then I would have left Dick to Janet Johnson. You know she was after him?"

"I suspected something like that," Peggy conceded.

"They'd probably be happily married by now and expecting their own baby."

"And what about you?"

"I should never have come home. I've brought nothing but disaster."

"But you did," Peggy insisted gently. "The damage is done. You're not a headstrong girl anymore. You can't just run away again. You're a young woman now, with responsibilities to your husband and the child that belongs to both of you."

"But Robin isn't. . . ." Kathy began to object.

"Yes. She's your child *and* Dick's, because he loves her and he loves you. If you'd come back to Springfield as a young widow with a baby, he would have married you and adopted Robin. It's no different now. He loves her like his own."

"But he doesn't even suspect. . . ." Kathy began to protest guiltily.

"You can't undo the past, Kathy, but you can build the future."

"I know the honest thing is to confess everything to Dick and suffer the consequences. I've meant to from the beginning, and then I think of Daddy. . . . Oh Peggy, what should I do?'' A sob caught in Kathy's throat and tears welled in her eyes.

For a long moment, Peggy didn't answer. She didn't like playing God with other people's lives, even those she loved like the family she'd never had. Then she replied slowly, "Love them both, Robin and Dick, as much as you can, and the rest will follow.''

Kathy shut her eyes tightly, unable to face even Peggy now. "I don't know if I'm strong enough to,'' she murmured.

"If you're not,'' Peggy warned, "there's only one thing you'll gain. The knowledge of how very lonely it is to have a heart full of love and no one to give it to.''

Outside, a thick layer of snow quilted the bare trees and roads and empty flowerbeds. The storm had stopped. Dusk had fallen over the town, and with it came the singular stillness that follows a snowstorm. Janet Johnson trudged home through the drifts, leaving her frozen car abandoned in the hospital parking lot. Outside her, the world seemed sunk in universal peace, but within, Janet's emotions were in turmoil. Day and night, her aching heart allowed her to think of only one thing.

She'd thought that the passage of time would make it easier to face Dick. But just the opposite had happened. Every time she saw him, it hurt that much more. If she didn't love him so much, she might let her discovery pass. But her heart and jealousy went too deep. If the baby was only one month premature, then it couldn't be

Dick's. The idea had festered and grown in her mind ever since she'd held Robin. She had to find out the truth, and when she did, she'd decide what to do with it. She didn't want to hurt Dick or the innocent baby. But Kathy Roberts. . . .

Janet would give anything to make Kathy Roberts crawl. The more she brooded, the more obsessed Janet became with evening the score with Kathy. Her boots ground into the virginal snow, leaving a path of footsteps in the streets as unwavering as her determination. Maybe Dick did have to marry Kathy, as virtually everybody in Springfield believed. Certainly, he was the kind of man who could always be counted on to do the honorable thing. Or maybe Kathy had been desperate to marry someone—anyone. Maybe she'd been running away. From what, though?

The pieces of the puzzle fit so easily: her sudden return, whirlwind courtship, and instant marriage. And now, just six months later, a baby, sturdier than any premature infant Janet had ever seen. Robin might be one month early, but not three. If she only knew what Kathy had been doing in New York. . . .

Janet trudged on, her quickening breath forming clouds of vapor in the black night. By the time she reached her own apartment door, the snowplows were beginning to clear the streets, creating mountains of snow on each side. Her mind was made up. If she couldn't investigate Kathy's mysterious past herself, she would hire someone who could. Dick had a right to know exactly what he'd married, Janet told herself, soothing her conscience as she dialed the number of Arlo Thomas, private investigator.

Chapter Nine

A Cruel Christmas

Dick stepped back and surveyed his handiwork, admiring the towering height and stately shape of the blue spruce he'd just put up in the window of the living room. The Christmas tree was a beauty—the biggest he could find in all of Springfield.

The room looked as though a cyclone had struck. Spruce boughs lopped off the bottom of the tree to make it fit the stand, a stack of packages wrapped in holiday paper, a hacksaw, boxes of bulbs, sheaves of tinsel, strings of lights, and garlands of laurel were strewn over the rug. But Dick faced the chaos happily. It was Robin's first Christmas, as well as the first for Kathy and him. And he wanted to make it wonderful.

Whistling "Jingle Bells," he set to work decorating the tree. By midnight, the cozy apartment had been transformed into a

Christmas wonderland. The tree sparkled with ornaments of every color, shimmering silver threads, and flickering blue lights. Laurel ropes were wound around every doorframe, and mistletoe dangled from the light fixture that hung in the center of the living room ceiling. Presents were piled beneath the tree, and in front of the fireplace hung three candy-striped stockings overflowing with Christmas surprises. One of the stockings was tiny enough to fit a doll. Tomorrow would be Christmas Eve, the day Robin and Kathy were coming home.

Exhausted but too excited to sleep, Dick sank into his favorite easy chair and sat admiring the decorations. He'd always loved Christmas, but this year was going to be more special than ever before. He could hardly wait to see Kathy's face when he brought her home in the morning. Meta had offered to come over and decorate, but Dick had refused. He wanted to do every bit himself for his new family.

The sun was already beaming on the blanket of snow outside when Dick stirred again. He opened his eyes and looked around in surprise, stretching his neck to work out the crick that had developed from sleeping all night in the chair. He'd only intended to sit down for a minute—the Christmas lights were still flickering on the tree. Glancing at his watch, Dick jumped up. He was due to pick up Kathy and Robin at ten o'clock, and he still had a dozen things to do.

"Ready, darling?" Dick burst into Kathy's room, barely able to contain his eagerness to have his wife and baby home at last. But the room was empty. A quick glance around revealed that it had been stripped of the little personal touches that had developed during Kathy's weeklong stay. He opened the closet door. Even her suitcase was gone. The knot of fear that had never totally dissolved hardened. His worst nightmare had come true—Kathy had gone away again.

Dick stood rooted by his loss. His first instinct was to go after her, chase her and bring her home. But he had no idea where she'd gone, or why. Then he thought of Robin. Rushing out, heedless of everything except the overwhelming need to see that Robin was safe, he ran to the nursery. If the baby were gone, too. . . . The pain was so intense, he couldn't think or feel beyond it. Inside, his heart was crying *Robin, Robin, Robin.*

Abruptly, he skidded to a halt and stared in disbelief. Relief washed over him like an oceanic wave. The nursery window was just ahead and standing in front of it, oblivious to everything except the baby they were peering at, stood Kathy and her father. Although Dick's feet had stopped, his heart was still racing when Kathy and Joe turned around.

"What's the matter, Dick?" Kathy asked in alarm when she saw him. "You look as though you just saw a ghost."

"Nothing. I'm fine, fine," he stammered. "I went to the room. You were gone. . . ." He was afraid he wasn't making any sense.

"We just walked over to see if Robin was ready to go home," Joe offered. He understood

Dick's fear exactly, because it haunted him as well. "I'm sorry if we gave you a scare."

"Where's your bag, Kathy? I looked in the closet. Even the suitcase was gone," Dick said apologetically. "I guess I sort of panicked."

"Meta took it out to the car," Joe explained, looking uneasily from Dick to his daughter. "Kathy called this morning and asked us to come over and bring her home."

"You knew I was coming, darling," Dick protested. "I admit I'm a few minutes late, but you couldn't possibly believe that I'd forget you and Robin."

"You don't understand, Dick." A pale and very tense Kathy interrupted. "Daddy's going to let me stay at his house—just until I get my strength back."

"But it's our first Christmas. I have everything ready." Dick felt like weeping. Ever since Robin's birth, Kathy had been acting like a total stranger. He thought of the magical tree and the bulging stockings.

"It will only be a few days, Dick. Don't make a big production of it," she lied. "You're away all day, and I'm afraid to be alone now. This way Meta will be right there to help me with Robin."

"We can hire a nurse, if that's what's bothering you," Dick offered hopefully.

Kathy's whole body stiffened. She couldn't go home with Dick—not bringing Bob Lang's baby in her arms. "I don't want to argue about it here," she objected. "Can't you at least wait until we get outside? I'm sure every nurse in the hospital is gossiping about us already without you giving them more ammunition for their malicious tongues."

Before he could respond, the nurse came out of the nursery carrying Robin swaddled snugly in a warm afghan. While Kathy was receiving the baby, Joe shuffled over and clapped Dick on the shoulder. "Give her a little while longer," he advised in a quiet undertone. "I know it's been tough on you, but she's gone through a pretty disruptive period ever since she came home to Springfield. We don't want to lose her again, especially now."

Dick shrugged dejectedly, knowing that there was nothing he could say. Kathy had defeated him once more. It was a frigid, blustery day. When they got outside, they wouldn't have the time or inclination to discuss the question further.

"Ready, boys?" Kathy turned, a bright smile painted on her pale face.

"Here, I'll carry Robin," Dick said, moving to take the baby.

"No," Kathy objected shrilly, hugging the warm bundle in her arms as if it might be snatched away at any moment. "I can manage myself."

Dick wheeled around without another word and started for the elevator. Trailing behind him with her father, Kathy shuddered involuntarily as they passed a patient with a face so hideously scarred that he looked more like a monster than a human. Peggy was helping him down the hall, but Kathy turned away and hurried by without a word. On the way downstairs, she chattered incessantly about everything and everyone that came to mind in a futile effort to lighten the heavy mood that weighed down all three of them.

"I have a wonderful Christmas present for you!" Bill's excited face was ruddy from the cold, and his arms were so full of packages that he staggered beneath his cumbersome load.

"Who do you think you are, Santa Claus? You look like you bought out the whole of Springfield." Bert didn't want to dampen Bill's exuberant spirits, but her stomach muscles knotted sickeningly as she helped him unload his bundles. She'd tramped through every store in town until she was bone weary from the ordeal, looking for bargains to keep their Christmas spending within the tight budget she'd set for them. "I thought we'd agreed to economize this year, so that we could put aside a little bit every week to pay off your debts." Toting up the cost of his extravagance in her mind, Bert couldn't completely contain her worry.

"Not anymore," Bill said, blithely brushing aside her concern. "This is for you." He thrust a florist's box in her arms. "And this is for Papa and the boys—a bucket of candy, chocolate, and peppermint stick mixed. The rest are for Christmas." He grinned down at Bert. "Well, what are you waiting for? Open it!"

Reluctantly, Bert lifted the lid and inhaled an intoxicating aroma. Nestled on a bed of green tissue paper was a spray of miniature golden orchids.

"They're beautiful," she murmured, lifting them almost reverently from the box. "But what are these presents for?"

"To celebrate," Bill beamed. "I'm giving up the insurance business. I don't have to moonlight anymore, and you don't have to pinch pennies. Sid and I have decided on a much better plan. It's a big step, but we think we're ready for it."

"That's wonderful!" Bert exclaimed, caught up in her husband's infectious enthusiasm. "Begin at the beginning and tell me all about it."

"There's not all that much to tell," Bill paused. "You know we've been planning to start a branch in New York. Well, Sid thinks I should open the office there. It will mean a lot more money—and the chance I need to make good again."

Bert had been relieved that Bill would be giving up his second job, until she heard his new proposal. "You mean you want to go to New York?" she blurted out.

"Don't worry, honey," he said, putting an arm around her and hugging her. "It's my big chance."

"No," she objected firmly. "Tell Sid he'll have to find someone else's husband to send. It's out of the question."

"I'll make you all proud of me. You'll see," Bill promised.

"I'm already proud of you—the whole family is," Bert insisted. "You don't have to prove anything to anyone. How can I make you believe that?"

"By standing by me," he answered quietly, "like you always have, instead of making it harder for me than it already is. And by explaining to the boys—especially to Mikey—why I have to do this."

The color drained from Bert's face and she held the spray of orchids up to her nose as if the heavenly aroma could revive her spirits. "You really are serious about this, Bill, aren't you?" she asked, dreading the answer she knew he would give.

"Dead serious. I've never been more set on anything in my life."

"All right, Bill. If you really feel that you have to do this, I won't stand in your way. On one condition," Bert paused and breathed deeply, gathering the courage she would need to bear the wrenching move, while Bill waited anxiously for her to continue.

"What is it? What do you want me to do, Bert?"

"Let the boys and me move to New York with you."

The words were barely out of her mouth before Bill gave his answer in adamant, unequivocal terms. "Absolutely not. It's out of the question."

"Well, I'm not letting you go alone." Bert dug in her heels and faced him squarely, her voice rising. "And that's final."

"I don't want to leave you, but there's no other way," he insisted. "We'll be able to save much more money if I go alone, and we won't upset the boys. Don't you see? We can't uproot them a second time in less than a year. It would be terrible for them—especially for Mikey, now that he's just getting started in another new school. And think of Papa. If we all went to

New York, he'd be left here alone. He's not getting any younger, you know, and the kids mean so much to him. They're his whole life now."

Bert turned away. She couldn't refute his arguments. But still, the thought of his leaving them filled her with a terrible dread. She knew all too well how Bill reacted under pressure and, without any tempering influence, she was afraid the old cycle of drinking would start again. But she couldn't admit that she didn't trust him to go to New York alone.

Bill came up behind her and put his arms around her. "It won't be forever, I promise. Just long enough to get us back on our feet. Then I'll turn the office over to someone else," he murmured.

She leaned back against him, her soft warmth pressed wearily against his familiar leanness. He was the only man she'd ever loved, and he was leaving her. The pain was like a knife turning in her heart.

"It's all because of Mikey, isn't it?" she said numbly. "You think you have to prove something to him, but going away isn't the answer. That won't prove anything. Mikey's too young to understand what you're trying to do. To him it will only mean that you're deserting him again."

For a long time, Bill didn't answer, then he said stubbornly, "All I know is that I have to do this. I'm counting on you to explain it to Mikey—to make him understand. I know you won't let me down. You never have."

"And Papa and Meta?"

"I'll tell them myself after the holidays."

"Oh, Bill!" Bert's voice caught in her throat and she cried out. "How can I let you go—just now when we were beginning to find each other again, trust each other, love each other."

Bill turned her around and wrapped her in his arms. "It will be hard on all of us for a while. But then we'll be together, really together," he vowed.

His breath was like a clear breeze against her cheek, and she gazed up at him, wanting to bury her dire forebodings in the warm flame of his eyes. She wanted to believe Bill, but she couldn't.

"Hold me, Bill, and kiss me," she pleaded, suddenly afraid that there would be too few times left for them.

He tilted her chin up and fitted his lips to hers in a kiss that swelled and burned like the first fire of their love. Bert's mouth answered his in a response more passionate than any he'd aroused in her through the long, rocky course of their marriage. She felt his body tremble, shaken by the unexpected ardor of her lips, and his kiss deepened, consuming her in its delirious hunger.

"When will the boys be home?" Bill murmured, drawing away reluctantly.

"Not for hours," she admitted. "Papa took them downtown to see the Christmas lights."

"Just what I was hoping to hear." He inhaled sharply, drawing his mouth along the sensitive column of her neck.

"Kiss me again," Bert begged, her body melding itself to his. This was the man she'd vowed her life to—heart, soul, and flesh—until death did they part. But even his kisses couldn't dispel the ominous thought that the parting he'd proposed had all the finality of death. Bert clung desperately to him as he carried her upstairs, the spray of delicate orchids crushed between them.

"I propose a toast." Dick raised his champagne glass and smiled across the table at his wife, who was feeding Robin. "To the best Christmas present I've ever had—and to her beautiful mother."

Kathy blushed and busied herself with the baby to avoid meeting her husband's eyes.

"I'll drink to that," Joe seconded proudly.

The warm glow of candlelight suffused the dining room. Meta had set the table with a festive green cloth and her best china and crystal, the only residue of her extravagant life with Ted White. A sterling silver bowl of holly and white roses formed a striking centerpiece.

"Well, it certainly has been a Christmas to remember," Laura Grant rejoined with a laugh. "Altogether too much excitement for my frail heart," she added, looking around the room with undisguised curiosity. She'd never been in the Roberts' house before, and she was frankly surprised. Meta had introduced subtle changes over the past few years, gradually transforming the comfortable chaos that Kathy had grown up with into a warm yet stylish home. The old furniture was dressed up in slipcovers of unbleached linen and natural shades of cotton. Rugs and pillows added the bright dashes of color that brought the rooms to vibrant life.

"No need to pull any of that fragile heart business in the present company," Dr. Grant boomed. His face was red from the champagne and cocktails, and his manner even more expansive than usual. "We all know what a tough old bird you really are, Laura."

"Honestly, Richard," Laura began petulantly.

But before she could go on, Meta had pushed back her chair and stood up, champagne glass poised for another toast. She hadn't expected to entertain the Grants for Christmas dinner—let alone take in Kathy and her baby. But now that she'd somehow managed to get through it gracefully, she wasn't about to let it end with a domestic squabble.

"To a man in a million." Meta smiled with genuine affection at Dick. "No baby could ever have a more loving father."

He blushed, embarrassed, as they all stood up. Everyone drank to the proud father— except one. Although Kathy raised her champagne glass to her lips, she only pretended to sip it. Robin had no father, and never would.

Abruptly excusing herself, she fled upstairs to her old room with the baby. In the morning, Dick could bring the new bassinet over. But for tonight, she and Robin would sleep together in her old bed.

Dick watched his wife's departing figure until it was out of sight. "Robin has had a long day," he apologized bleakly. "And Kathy, too."

Meta forced a holiday gaiety into her voice, hoping to dispel the threatening cloud descending over her Christmas party. "Why don't we all go into the living room for coffee? Once we begin opening the presents, I'm sure Kathy will be down again."

"You can bet on that," Joe backed her up enthusiastically. "No one loves surprises more than Kathy."

"She's certainly given us a few," Dr. Grant snorted sarcastically.

"Really, Richard." Laura shot him a baleful glance. "It is Christmas, whatever we may feel."

Dick was too dispirited to even notice his parents' snide exchange. He went upstairs to get Kathy when they started to open the presents that were piled in extravagant abundance under the silver and blue tree. But he came back alone.

Christmas Day came and went, and the candy-striped stockings he'd brought over from his apartment still lay unopened under the Roberts' tree.

Chapter Ten

A House Divided

The new year dawned bleakly. In Washington, Harry S. Truman was sworn in for his own term as president, leaving the pollsters and pundits eating crow. They'd been so certain he'd go down in defeat that newspapers had gone to press on election night with pictures of a grinning Dewey on page one. Around the country, shock waves over the sensational *Kinsey Report* were still reverberating. And on the radio, "Our Gal Sunday," the orphan girl from the little mining town of Silver Creek, Colorado, was still trying to find happiness as the wife of a wealthy and titled Englishman.

Lowering the radio to a whisper, Meta reached for the phone. She'd been forced to hang up on Bill when he called because she'd been in the midst of mixing a fresh batch of formula for Robin. Of course it was Kathy's job, but if Meta didn't do it, the poor baby would go hungry, she thought with mounting irritation.

Tension crackled in the Roberts' house like an electric current. Robin was already a month old, and still Kathy made no move to go home to her own apartment. Ignoring Meta's broad hints, she clung to her father as if she had become an infant again, instead of a mother. The uneasy peace that had existed between the two women throughout Kathy's pregnancy was shattered, and now the antagonism, always so close to the surface, erupted at the slightest provocation.

Both women were churning with volcanic emotions. While she was fond of the baby, Meta resented having her home taken over by her stepdaughter. She felt as if she'd been reduced to the demeaning role of maid. Kathy, still distraught and unable to see any way out of her dilemma, relied on her unsuspecting father like a compass in a storm. Without him, she would be totally lost—only she couldn't admit it to anyone, least of all Meta. And so the resentment festered and swelled, until life in the Roberts' house bore the earmarks of a battlefield front line. Joe and Dick were the hapless, innocent prisoners in an undeclared war.

"Bill, I can't believe you're really going through with this . . . this crazy move," Meta murmured into the phone. "All along I felt sure you'd come to your senses. Instead you're telling me that your bags are packed and you're actually prepared to walk out on your family, all because of some money that I don't need or want."

She paused to wave to Dick who'd just let

himself in, as he did now every day. Visiting rights were all that Kathy allowed him. Meta's plaintive voice followed him up the stairs. He walked heavily, like a man under a life sentence. The strain of their "arrangement" was beginning to tell.

"It's not too late to reconsider, Bill. All you have to do is tell Sid you changed your mind. You can always find somebody else. Think of what happened to me when I went to New York . . . and Joe. Believe me, it's a brutal town." The only one who'd survived it was Kathy, Meta thought, and she was a hundred times tougher than Bill would ever be.

Dick closed the door to Kathy's room behind him, shutting out Meta's urgent plea as completely as Bill did. Robin was lying on the bed, waving her fat legs in the air as if she'd just made a marvelous discovery—her toes. Dick broke into a beaming smile at the wondrous sight. No matter how many times he saw her, and touched her, and fed her, and changed her, the miracle of his baby daughter never dimmed.

"How are you today?" Dick sat down at the foot of the bed beside Kathy and leaned over to kiss her.

She turned her face so that his lips brushed her cheek, instead of her mouth. "Fine, except for Meta," she pouted. "She's always on my back about something or other. You know what I think, Dick? She doesn't like Robin one bit more than she likes me. I have a good mind to tell Daddy how she treats us when he's not home."

Dick sighed deeply. The joy that had filled

him when he saw his wife and child was seeping away all too quickly. "Did it ever occur to you that it may not be all one-sided?" he said tightly, trying to control his irritation. "Maybe you've outstayed your welcome."

"You always take her side," Kathy complained crossly. "If you like her so much, why don't you stay downstairs and talk to her?"

"She was busy—fixing Robin's formula," he added pointedly. "That's right!" He reached over and tickled the bottom of Robin's foot, shifting his attention away from Kathy. "Do you know what your grandmother's doing? She's making bottles for you—lots and lots of bottles."

His fingers were walking up her leg. Robin laughed and waved her arms happily. Enchanted as always, Dick gathered her up in his arms and nuzzled her belly playfully. He found her utterly irresistible. "So what have you been doing with yourself all day? Missing your dad?"

Robin jabbed at his mouth with a plump finger, and he caught it in his mouth, kissing it and pretending to eat it. Watching them, Kathy wondered if she could ever love her daughter as much as Dick did. The thought was like a stab of pain, and she turned away. She couldn't bear to watch them together.

"Are you hungry, little bird?" Dick was asking the baby. "Do you want a bottle?"

"Probably," Kathy answered for her. "There's one in the bassinet she didn't finish. I'll get it," she offered, reaching out to take her child back. But Dick was already on his feet.

"It's all right," he assured her. "I like to feed

my little girl, don't I?" He planted a kiss on the tip of Robin's nose. When she gurgled happily, he planted another, and another.

Getting the bottle, he settled down in the rocking chair with her nestled comfortably in the crook of his arm and positioned a clean diaper under her chin to catch any dribbles of milk. Nothing in the world gave him more pleasure than caring for her.

"You certainly were hungry, weren't you?" Dick murmured as Robin sucked at the nipple greedily. "Well, don't worry, there's plenty more where this came from. Your grandmother just made a dozen fresh bottles for you," he said, holding her up on his shoulder to burp her.

"I wish you'd stop referring to Meta as her grandmother," Kathy complained petulantly. "She's nothing to me or to my baby." She knew she sounded unreasonable, but she couldn't help herself. Seeing Dick with Robin made her nervous and ashamed. She had to lash out at someone, and Meta was the readiest target.

With infinite tenderness, Dick cradled Robin in his arms again. The baby had dozed off on his shoulder. She looked angelic when she slept, he thought lovingly, as he laid her gently down in the bassinet and tucked the blanket around her.

"What do you want me to call her—that woman?" he teased. Crossing the room, he came back and sat down on the bed beside Kathy again.

But she was in no mood for joking. "You don't have to call her anything," she snapped.

"If she knew what was good for her, she'd pack her bags and get out of here."

"And so should I?" Dick asked sharply. He'd drawn a blank shade over his emotions so that Kathy couldn't read what was in his heart.

Instinctively, she reached out to him, touching his sleeve with her fingertips. The long, pink nails were perfectly manicured. Kathy had little else to occupy her time with. She could spend only so long bathing, dressing, diapering, and feeding Robin. "I didn't say that," she murmured.

"No," he admitted readily, "but that's what you were thinking. It's what you've wanted for a long time."

"No, never!" she protested. "How can you even think such an awful thing?"

Dick laughed grimly. "Easy—especially when I go home to a dark, empty house every night and lie in bed alone with nothing to hold but your cold pillow."

Anguish filled Kathy's wide violet eyes. "I'm sorry it's so awful for you, Dick. Sorrier than you'll ever understand. But I can't help it."

"Of course you can." He took her hand and pressed it tightly between both of his, encouraged by her sorrowful expression. Maybe she did care after all, he thought with a rush of hope. "You can come home with me— right now, today. All you have to do is put your coat on and bundle up Robin."

He got up to go to the closet, demonstrating just how simple it was, but Kathy tugged at his arm to hold him back. "No, stop it!" she cried. "I can't. You don't understand."

He turned back and stared at her, stunned by the desperate passion in her voice. "Why not?" he demanded as evenly as he could. "Just tell me that much. Let me help you, at least," he pleaded.

Kathy shrank away from him as if he possessed a dangerous poison that would destroy her on contact. "Maybe tomorrow, Dick. Let's wait and see how I feel. I still get so tired. . . ." She yawned to emphasize her point. The remote mask she'd adopted to keep him at a distance since Robin's birth was once again securely in place.

"That's what you said yesterday, and the day before, and last week," Dick protested. His patience was running out. He knew that many women suffered postpartum depression after childbirth. It was a common enough phenomenon, but that didn't make it any easier to cope with. As a doctor, he knew he shouldn't press Kathy. But he was a man, too.

"I love you, Kathy," he blurted. Unable to hold back the rush of emotion that surged within him, he seized her by the shoulders and pulled her up into his arms. "Doesn't that mean anything to you anymore?"

Kathy trembled, excited by the unexpected contact, as Dick's body pressed tighter against hers. Suddenly, her heart was racing and her lips were dry. She had to moisten them with the pointed tip of her tongue before she could form the words that she wanted him to hear—and to remember always.

"It means everything, Dick. That's the whole trouble. You have to believe me." She gazed up at him, imploring him to perform the impossible act of faith, and he saw her desire, as deep as his own, reflected in the liquid mirror of her eyes.

"I'm trying to," he murmured. He was keenly aware of her silken hair brushing his cheek, her sweet breath coming in sharp, quick gasps on his neck, her hands pressing him close to her. "But you make it so hard. I need you, Kathy. I need you to be with me, to be my wife," he tried to say, but his urgent words were engulfed in the intoxicating taste of her soft, full lips.

Kathy had denied him so long that now the mere touch of her fingers, the whisper of her lips, was enough to inflame his wildest passions. Dick felt as if he'd come through a scorching desert to feast at the oasis of her lips. Was it a mirage or was it true? What he'd longed for and wept for was really happening. He was holding his wife in his arms again, and she was answering his deepest hunger with her own.

For a fraction of a second, Kathy tried to struggle against the tidal wave of desire sweeping through her, but her body was already betraying her. Her lips parted to receive him hungrily. She moved sensually against the rocklike plain of his chest as his hands roamed possessively over her body, rediscovering the swells and eddies that held him in thrall. Kathy knew she should stop him, but she couldn't bear to have the delirious feelings end. He was raining kisses all over her face, down the pale curve of her neck, releasing buttons and hooks with dangerous abandon so that his lips could continue their downward journey. Nothing could stop Dick now, until he possessed her again, totally and completely.

In a burst of searing clarity, Kathy realized that she couldn't let him do it—no matter how urgently they both wanted it. She couldn't compound her treachery by falling into his arms now. No matter how desperately she hungered to be engulfed in his passion and forget everything in the glorious release of lovemaking, she knew she had to stop him if she still could.

"No, Dick, stop!" she cried, pushing against him with all her strength, but he wouldn't release her.

Dick was like a man possessed. He couldn't control himself. He would have her. "You're my wife," he breathed heavily. "You want me as much as I want you, Kathy, you know you do."

"No," she cried again, but he could only hear the pounding of his own heart. He pushed her back so that she lost her balance and sprawled on the bed. For an instant he stared at her. Her blouse was open, exposing the round spheres of her breasts. Her skirt was twisted up, allowing her milky thighs to gleam enticingly. Then he fell on her, covering her body.

Kathy struggled, but she knew she was fighting a losing battle. She couldn't stop him, but at least she wouldn't help him, she vowed. She lay like a statue, as if life had suddenly drained out of her, until it was over as suddenly as it had begun.

Sick with disgust and self-loathing, Dick rolled away from her. Can a husband rape his own wife? he thought. The tempestuous desire that had engulfed him a moment before had burned out, leaving him feeling empty and charred. What had he been thinking of? What madness had seized him? Adjusting his clothes, he stumbled out blindly and started down the stairs. Kathy still lay crumpled on the bed where he'd left her, but he couldn't bear to look back at her. Dimly, he heard Robin begin to cry as if some primitive instinct were warning her that he was abandoning her, but even that didn't make him stop.

In the kitchen, Meta heard the front door slam and thought with surprise that Dick must have gone without even stopping to say a word. Pulling back the curtain, she peered out the window and saw him rushing down the walk. Either he was in a big hurry or he'd had a blow-up with Kathy, she thought curiously. Letting the curtain drop again, she turned back to the vegetable soup she was beginning and found Kathy framed in the kitchen door.

"Do you have a bottle ready?" she asked curtly. "Robin's hungry again."

"That's not my fault," Meta snapped. "If it weren't for me, the child would be starving. Why don't you take care of your own baby?"

"I would," Kathy retorted, "if you'd get out of my way long enough."

Meta stared at her stepdaughter's flushed, insolent face and felt her blood begin to boil. "This is my house—and my kitchen. And don't you ever forget it," she warned.

Kathy, overwrought by her encounter with Dick, lashed back at Meta. "It will always be my house as long as Daddy is alive, and you know it. I'm sick of having you interfere with my life. You were spying on Dick just now. And don't try to deny it because I caught you."

Meta, still upset about Bill's decision, lost her temper completely. "Get out of here," she cried, hurling a bottle across the room. Kathy ducked and the bottle crashed against the door, sending glass and formula splattering over the walls and floor.

"You're a crazy woman," Kathy screamed, "just like that jury said. Insane! Only they should have had you committed because there's nothing temporary about it. When I tell my father about this, he'll have you put away for good—locked up so that you can never disrupt our lives again. You almost killed me. You *are* a murderess!"

"Get out!" Meta screamed hoarsely. Her dark eyes glowed eerily from deep caverns in her face that had turned the color of ash at Kathy's onslaught. Brandishing the stockpot she'd been filling, she rushed at Kathy, sending carrots, celery, and onion slices flying in every direction. But before she could reach her, Kathy grabbed a baby bottle and ran, not stopping until she was safely back upstairs in her own room.

Meta slumped down hopelessly on the stairs as the door slammed, shutting out the sound of Robin's persistent wailing.

"You have to do something, Joe." Meta confronted him before he'd even had time to close the door. "I don't care what mysterious traumas your daughter has suffered, it's just not healthy living like this."

Joe leaned over and kissed her on the forehead. "I know it's been said many times, many ways, but you're beautiful when you're angry."

Meta refused to be deflected. "Flattery won't get you anywhere, Joe Roberts. I'm serious this time."

"Serious about what now?" Joe sighed. He was tired. Even though he didn't go to work until ten o'clock, being back at the paper full time was more exhausting than he'd anticipated, and he wasn't up for an argument.

"Kathy, of course. How can she ever iron out her problems—whatever they are—when she's living across town from her husband? It's not fair to Dick, or to Robin. They *are* a family, after all, and a family should be together."

"And it's not fair to you," Joe added sarcastically.

"Yes, that too," Meta admitted hotly. For once, she wouldn't back down. "She wrecked our life once already, and I won't let her do it again."

Joe walked heavily into the den. His limp, usually hardly noticeable, was pronounced now. "I'm sorry you haven't been happy with me, Meta. But Kathy is my daughter, and I'm not going to turn her out on the street. As far as I'm concerned, this will always be her home as long as I live."

Tears of anger and frustration sprang into Meta's eyes. "And what about me? Don't I count for anything?" she demanded. "Or am I just supposed to be the maid here? The chief cook and bottle-washer," she added cuttingly.

"You're my wife," he replied flatly, "even though you've regretted it for a long time."

"I've never regretted loving you," Meta cried. Joe always had a way of turning any argument back against her.

"Only marrying me." He stared at her with the cool gray-green eyes that always possessed the power to bore through to her soul. "Go ahead and say it. I know it's true."

"No!" Meta cried fiercely. "I won't let you do this to me, Joe. We're talking about Kathy and Dick, and I won't let you twist my meaning around, just because you're cleverer with words than I am. Think of Dick, if you don't care about my feelings. What kind of life is he having?"

"I know exactly how Dick feels—as a man and as a doctor." A cutting edge that Meta had heard only once before sharpened Joe's voice. Meta shuddered at the memory. He was slow to anger, but when he did, his rage was cold and implacable. She was the hot-blooded one in the family, and Joe the cool, levelheaded one. "He doesn't think it would be wise to push Kathy just now," he said. "She's been coming around since the baby was born, but she still needs time."

"And you intend to give it to her by allowing her to disrupt our life again, after I've worked so hard to rebuild it?" Meta shouted. "Can't you see what she's doing? What she's always tried to do? She still resents me, and she'll do anything in her power to drive us apart. This is just another despicable tactic to drive a wedge between us."

She'd been trying to keep her voice down so that she wouldn't wake up the baby, but she didn't care anymore. Her fury, once unleashed, was too deep to restrain. It rankled her that both Joe and Dick still persisted in defending Kathy and making excuses for her.

Turning his back on his wife's anger, Joe went over to the bar and began mixing himself a drink. He wished he had a cigarette, but Dick had made him give up smoking after his heart attack. The ice clinked in the glass, a jarring sound in the highly charged silence that gaped between them. He took a long drink and faced Meta. His voice was even, but an Arctic chill filled his eyes. Meta shivered, as if the temperature in the room had dropped suddenly, but Joe's words burned like acid in her heart.

"If that's true, Meta, and this is all some kind of ploy on Kathy's part, then you're playing right into her hands."

Meta wanted to tell him that Dick had been upstairs all afternoon, pleading with Kathy to go home, but she hesitated a moment too long. The doorbell rang—like a gong announcing the end of round one, Joe thought tiredly. Watching his wife as she debated whether to answer the bell or let it ring, he wondered, not for the first time, if marriage to Meta had been a mistake. Until then, Kathy had been so happy and carefree.

The bell pealed again insistently, and Meta turned away, leaving the situation more unresolved than ever. Joe listened impassively as her falsely bright, welcoming voice wafted in from the foyer.

"How do you do? So pleased to meet you, Mrs. Regan. Kathy is upstairs resting, but I'm sure she'll be delighted to see an old friend. Let me show you the way."

Her mouth drawn in a frigid smile, Meta started up the stairs. Her tall, stately figure formed a striking contrast to the woman who followed dutifully. Though only a year or two older, Peggy Regan had the look of a kindly matron. Her figure, always inclined to plumpness, had begun to spread, and the thick tweed suit and practical walking shoes she wore heightened the overall effect. Her dark hair, sprinkled with the first threads of gray, was cut and permed, creating a frizzled frame around her broad, kindly face. There was nothing false or contrived in her appearance. She was exactly what she appeared to be—not exciting or provocative, but simply a good, solid woman. Meta imagined her with a sturdy husband and a brood of freckled-faced children, never suspecting for a moment that she and Peggy Regan were in love with the same man. It was a secret that Peggy held fast in her heart, the reason for her anguished loneliness.

Glancing back over her shoulder hoping for a glimpse of Joe, she followed Meta, chatting animatedly the whole while about the happy days when she used to come to the Roberts' house to babysit for Kathy.

"I guess you know the way yourself, then," Meta interrupted. "Kathy's back in her old room—permanently, it looks like. First door at the top of the stairs to refresh your memory. Go ahead, Mrs. Regan." She stepped aside with a short, grating laugh. "I'm sure Kathy would rather see your face than mine."

Peggy looked at Meta, her bland expression revealing neither censure nor agreement. She had no intention of becoming embroiled in a battle of wills between these two very forceful women. "Thank you, Mrs. Roberts." She smiled sweetly. "And it's Miss Regan, though I hope you'll call me Peggy. Everyone does."

"I'll bring some tea up, Peggy. I'm sure Kathy will be glad to see a friendly face for a change," Meta added, her smile glued firmly in place.

When Peggy knocked and opened the door, she found the room sunk in shadows. Kathy was sitting in front of the window, rocking Robin, the sadness in her face silhouetted against the gathering dusk. A sorrowful madonna, Peggy thought, and her heart went out to her almost-daughter. Evidently, Kathy hadn't heard her knock, because she didn't look up but continued to rock, crooning softly to her baby.

"It's awfully glum in here without any lights. If Robin's not sleeping, I'll just turn on the bedside lamp," Peggy said brightly. "I remember you never did like the dark."

"Peggy!" Kathy looked up in surprise. "Where did you come from?"

"I just keep popping up like a genie, don't I?" she laughed as she turned on the light, chasing the shadows from the familiar room.

Except for the addition of the rocking chair and a bassinet, it still bore the earmarks of a young girl's room. Nothing had changed: the same old photos, just a little more faded, stuck in the dressing table mirror; the same books, a little dustier; the same mementos of special dates and dances, looking forlorn now.

"Actually," Peggy went on with deceptive casualness, "I bumped into Dick at the hospital. When I mentioned that I'd like to drop by the apartment to see how you and Robin were doing, he told me to come over here." She plopped down on the bed, just like she used to whenever Kathy was in the mood for a heart-to-heart talk, and studied her closely: the usually smiling mouth turned down glumly; the once sparkling eyes filled with sorrow; the smooth, pink cheeks now pale and stained with tears. Robin whimpered in her arms, as if her mother's sadness had infected her, too.

"Don't you think it's time you went home, where you belong, Kathy?" Peggy suggested softly.

"I am home," Kathy insisted stubbornly.

"No, not anymore. You're not a little girl now, no matter how much you wish you were, or could be again. You're a woman, and you belong with your husband."

"I thought you were on my side, but you sound just like the others," Kathy snapped back defensively. "They all want me to leave, except Daddy—and it's his house."

"Of course he doesn't want you to leave." Peggy's voice was as soothing as a caress. "In your father's eyes, you'll always be his little girl, even when you're a grandmother. But you can't fool yourself that easily. No matter how hard you try, you can't pretend that you are anymore. You have your own little girl now. You're not being fair to her, or to Dick—or to your father, no matter what he may say. Judging from the way your stepmother looked when she opened the door, your presence is putting a terrible strain on his marriage, as well as your own."

"Meta's just awful—there's nothing new about that. Daddy would be well rid of her. I hope she does pack her bags and. . . ."

A sharp knock at the door made Kathy bite her tongue.

"I hope I'm not interrupting anything," Meta's voice dripped with sarcasm, "but I thought Miss Regan—pardon me, Peggy— would like some tea." She placed a charmingly arranged silver tray on the bureau and turned abruptly to leave. "Don't hesitate to help yourself, Peggy. Kathy won't have the strength to serve you. You see, her childbirth—which you do realize was infinitely more difficult than any woman's since Eve—has left her utterly helpless. I doubt if she's even capable of lifting a teaspoon, let alone a cup."

"You witch!" Kathy shouted. But Meta was too quick for her. Both Kathy's words and the empty baby bottle she hurled after them fell on the closing door.

Allowing Kathy's anger time to burn itself out, Peggy busied herself serving the tea. It was a soothing drink. The steamy brew, with its subtle fragrance, seemed to exert a relaxing effect on the most difficult situations, and she had no desire to act as referee in a fight that could only have losers.

She stirred the milk in her tea, watching it cloud the clear, golden water. "Have you looked in the mirror lately, Kathy?" she began thoughtfully. "I mean really looked at yourself? Because, I think if you did, you'd see how selfishly you're behaving."

"No!" Kathy began to protest, but Peggy wouldn't be stopped.

"Yes," she insisted, determined to be heard. "After we talked in the hospital, I thought you were really going to try to make the best of your difficult situation—for Dick's sake and for Robin's, if not for your own. You were always a fighter. You never used to give up, because you were confident that if you tried hard enough, you could do it. Be a cheerleader. Get an A in Math. Whatever it was. . . . What's happened to you, Kathy? You've closed yourself up here in this musty old room so that you can feel as sorry for yourself as you like. You're clinging to a past you can never go back to, instead of starting to build a new life. You could have a real family, and a very happy one. You have all the ingredients—a husband and wife, a child, and, most essential of all, a deep reservoir of love to draw on."

But Peggy's encouraging words fell on deaf ears. Kathy was shaking her head hopelessly. "I can't," she cried. "You don't understand, Peggy. I can't! I just can't! When I married Dick, I thought I had gotten everything I wanted and needed—a name for my baby and respectability. But it's not enough." She paused for a moment, too wracked with guilt to speak.

"I'm living a lie, and I can't bear it," she blurted. "I didn't love Dick when I married him. Of course I was fond of him—I always have been—and I knew he was just as crazy about me as he'd always been. So I grabbed him. But since then, being with him every day so close. . . ." she faltered. "Oh, Peggy, I love him so much now, I can't even begin to describe it. And each time I see him, it makes me love him so much more that I can't bear it." Tears sprang to her eyes as she thought of him.

"For heaven's sake, Kathy, that's nothing to cry about," Peggy said. "Why, any girl, myself included, would give the world to have a love like that."

"You don't understand," Kathy cried in frustration. "It's not wonderful at all. It's terrible. Now, every time I see him bend over Robin so full of pride and tenderness, it tears my heart out. If I didn't love him so much, I wouldn't care. But watching him with her makes me realize that what I've done to him is wrong, horribly wrong. I can't stand to face him any longer, yet the thought of living without him now is just as impossible."

"That's the most important thing to remember," Peggy insisted. "That and how much you love each other, and how much you both love Robin. Go home, Kathy, while you still can," she pleaded. "It won't be easy for you, but then, it's never easy. If you look just a little way below the surface, you'll discover that nobody has a charmed life. In fact, sometimes when you stop and consider someone else's troubles, your own problems don't look nearly as bad by comparison. Give that some thought.

"There's a patient in the hospital right now I'm taking care of," she went on, hoping her story would help Kathy put her own conflicting emotions in perspective. "A man named Dan Peters. His face is so hideously disfigured that I have to force myself not to turn away in revulsion every time I look at him. But he hasn't given up. Not at all. He's going to have plastic surgery and, if it's successful he'll be able to have a new life, too.

"People are beginning again every day, turning their backs on their mistakes and starting fresh." Peggy spoke earnestly, trying with all her heart to reach Kathy before it was too late and her marriage was destroyed beyond repair. "You can, too. No matter how tough it is for you, you owe it to Dick to at least try."

"Do you really think it's not too late?" Kathy's eyes met hers with burning intensity, her future, her happiness hanging in the question. And Peggy knew she had to answer as honestly as she could.

"Not if you really love him so much as you say you do," she replied firmly.

"And it's not. . . ." Kathy faltered. "Not cheating Dick somehow?"

"The only thing you can cheat him out of now is love." Peggy smiled wistfully. "And that's the worst cheat of all. Take it from one who knows."

"Then I'll try, Peg. I really will. I'll go home tomorrow before I lose my courage. I promise," Kathy swore, and her eyes shone for the first time since Robin was born. "Maybe I'll surprise

Dick. I can just see his face." She laughed with an uncontainable burst of happiness.

But that night Robin woke up vomiting and with a fever. And Kathy waited to go home until the virus passed, giving Janet Johnson just enough time to wreak her cruel, supremely clever revenge.

Chapter Eleven

Drastic Steps

Papa Bauer shuffled his feet to keep out the numbing cold and slipped his arm through his daughter's. The groundhog had seen its shadow, and the old wives' tale had come true. Two added weeks of the most unforgiving winter weather had descended upon them, further dampening the bleak spirits of the desolate group that huddled together in the Springfield train station. Even sheltered within the terminal, people found the cold merciless.

"You look so tired, Meta," he said, reading the strain in his daughter's handsome face. "What is troubling you?"

"It's nothing, Papa." She brushed aside his concern. "I hate the winter, you know that. And I hate losing Bill."

"It won't be forever." He murmured the empty words, knowing as he did that they held no consolation. Although they'd never discussed it, he knew that both Meta and Bert shared his fears for his generous-hearted, weak-willed son.

"Long enough," she muttered darkly. "New York will devour Bill. I should know. Remember what it did to me, and I'm a lot tougher."

"You were only a girl then, so innocent and impulsive." A faraway look misted Papa's eyes at the memory of the time and event that had altered their lives irredeemably.

It was so many years ago that Meta had run away without a word to anyone, and yet Papa remembered it as painfully as though it were yesterday. Mama had never recovered from the shock of losing her eldest daughter. By the time Meta had come home, like a wounded, frightened bird bringing with her their first grandchild, Mama was already dead. Would she still be alive now if Meta had never left Springfield? Mama had been so strong. He had never expected to lose her like that. But it was as if her heart had broken when Meta walked out, and there was nothing the doctors could do to put it together again.

Papa shook his head. So much sorrow, he thought sadly. Such bitter losses. First Mama. He missed her still, as if a part of him—the best part—had been carved out of his body. Her death had left a void in his life that nothing would ever fill. And then Chuckie. When Ted White came to town looking for his son, Papa had pressed Meta to marry him. The guilt still weighed heavily in his heart. He blamed himself for Chuckie's death and for the grief and violence that had almost destroyed Meta. When she'd finally married Joe, he prayed that she would find a measure of peace and contentment. But judging from the way she looked, Papa thought, her marriage was creating new problems for her.

Huddling deeper inside her fur coat, Meta looked anxiously over at Joe. Although Robin was just getting over a virus, he'd insisted on bringing her to the station with them to see Bill off. He claimed that Kathy needed a couple of hours of undisturbed rest, but Meta knew that wasn't the real reason. Joe just couldn't resist an opportunity to show off his granddaughter, even if she contracted pneumonia in the process.

He was hunkered down now in the middle of the railroad station so that Mikey could see the baby. Although Robin was dressed so warmly that only her big blue eyes, button nose, and rosebud mouth were visible, the little boy was examining her intently. Summoning all his courage, Mikey reached out a tentative finger to touch her cheek and make sure she was real. He knew she was supposed to be his cousin, but she looked so much like a doll. Somehow Robin managed to free her hand of the clothing and blankets that encased her. Gurgling happily, she grasped Mikey's finger and refused to let go. Without understanding why, Mikey began to smile, and he couldn't stop.

"Talk to her, Mikey," Joe urged gently, "and she'll talk back. Not words, of course, just happy, cooing sounds."

Mikey's cheeks flushed in confusion. "What should I say?"

"Whatever you feel like. Just hearing your voice will make her happy," Joe encouraged.

"Do you mean it?" the boy asked uncertainly.

"Try it," Joe urged.

"Hello, little baby," Mikey began timidly, but as Robin cooed and laughed, delighted by the attention, he began to relax and talk more freely. "My name's Michael Bauer. I'm your cousin—well, sort of your cousin, anyway—and if anyone's ever mean to you, you just tell me and I'll fix him good," Mikey promised earnestly.

All he could think of was that she liked him, she really liked him. No one ever had, except Papa Bauer. Not even his mother and father. It didn't matter to him that Robin was only a baby, or that she didn't know who he was, because he was making her happy just by being with her. It was a heady new sensation that made Mikey want to laugh out loud with joy. He was glad he'd come to the station after all.

"May I hold her?" he ventured, even though he was positive the answer would be no.

"Sure," Joe said easily. "This old arm could use a rest," he added, carefully transferring Robin to Mikey's eager arms. "She's a lot heavier than she looks. Just be careful to hold her head up. Babies aren't strong enough to do that for themselves, you know."

While Meta watched them anxiously from across the station, fearful every second that Mikey would drop the baby, Bert observed the scene with a full heart.

She could scarcely believe her eyes. Mikey was usually like a stone wall, unmoved by either discipline or praise. Nothing seemed to touch him. He lived in their home like an enemy force, his sullen silence invading the happiness they had tried so hard to restore. Bert was sure that more than the money he owed, Bill felt driven by Mikey's hostility to go to New York. But she was powerless to do anything about it. Mikey's emotions were locked up so tight she couldn't reach them. Even when he was branded a thief and expelled from school, he didn't show any sign of remorse. He retained the same stony silence with which he met everything—anger, love, or threats. Most disturbing of all, they were beginning to get the same negative reports about him from the new school he'd started in: disruptive behavior in the classroom, an antagonistic attitude toward the teachers and other children, and a total disinterest in his schoolwork. Mikey seemed to be carrying a colossal chip on his shoulder that nothing could dislodge. The new principal was advising professional help for the boy unless some dramatic improvement occurred.

Bert was grateful, at least, that Bill's last glimpse of his son would be of a smiling face filled with love. Up to the last minute, she hadn't been sure that Mikey would even come to the station, but Papa Bauer's gentle persuasion had worked the necessary miracle. Mikey had accompanied them, although he had tagged behind, resentful and brooding, the entire way. It had been so long since Bert had seen his face wreathed in smiles, she almost couldn't believe it was her son playing with the Roberts' grandchild.

Bert reached out for her husband's hand, blinking hard to hold back the tears, and prayed that Bill would remember Mikey the way he looked right now. Bill twisted, shifting the weight of his youngest son who was perched on his shoulders, and squeezed Bert's hand so hard it ached. "Hang on, old girl, we're almost there." His voice broke.

Bert looked up and saw that his eyes glistened with the tears he was holding back. Did Bill feel it, too? she wondered. She couldn't ask him now, even if she'd wanted to. Arizona hadn't been the end of their marriage. But this parting was. Bert knew it instinctively. United we stand, divided we fall, she thought bleakly. The Bauer family would never be the same again.

"Do you think the boys will forget me?" he blurted suddenly. The last time he'd stood in this station was when he had brought Mikey on that rainy, disappointing day to see President Truman on his whistle-stop tour.

"Not a chance of it." Bert forced a brightness into her voice even though it sounded false to her own ears. "Anyway, you promised it wouldn't be forever."

"The four twenty-eight arriving on track one. Passengers only are allowed to board." The stationmaster's twang filled the station like the voice of doom. The whistle of the silver engine sounded. Steam hissed and great clouds of smoke billowed as the train descended on them. Then, all of a sudden, everyone was rushing forward. Bill slipped little Billy off his shoulders and wrapped Bert in his arms. She clung to him as if she'd never let go, and felt the taste of his last kiss lingering until the train pulled away.

Watching it with a heavy heart until it disappeared down the track, Bert wondered if Mikey had said goodbye to his father. In the last-minute scramble of bags and hurried embraces, she'd lost sight of her son.

Driving home from the station, Meta was uncharacteristically quiet. In spite of the big send-off, she was sure Papa shared her fears about Bill.

Meta stared out of the car window fixedly. "Bert's a fool," she murmured. "She should never have let Bill go . . . but he's so stubborn."

"I thought it was a big promotion for him, and quite a feather in the cap of Benson and Bauer to be opening up an office in New York," Joe said.

Meta scowled. "That's the line Bill's been giving everybody. But I didn't expect you to fall for it. He needs the extra money to pay Papa and me back what we loaned him when he was so down and out. We both told him not to. We'd rather have him here where he belongs than all the money in Fort Knox. But you know how Bill is. Once he gets his mind set on something, there's no shaking him. He's got some ridiculous notion that his honor and integrity are at stake."

"Well," Joe advised philosophically, "it may be good for him to get out on his own. He's a grown man and he's never been out of Springfield in his life, has he? The change may be just what he needs."

Meta glared at him with barely veiled hostility. "Was it just what *you* needed?" she challenged hotly. "Look what New York did to you. When you got home from your wild-goose chase in New York you were. . . ."

"I know," Joe interrupted curtly. "You don't have to rub it in. I know I've disappointed you."

Meta bit her lip. She didn't want to get into another argument with Joe. "Bert should have gone with him, and taken the boys, too," she murmured tensely.

"What did you say?" Joe glanced over at her anxiously, then quickly slammed his foot on the brake as a car cut across in front of them to turn. "That woman should have her license revoked," he growled angrily. If he'd been alone, he simply would have leaned hard on the horn. But with such precious cargo along, he couldn't afford to be lenient with careless drivers.

Clutching Robin tighter, Meta craned her neck around to get a better look at the offending driver. "Wasn't that Janet Johnson, the nurse Dick used to date?"

"Whoever the hell she is, she's going to get someone killed driving like that," Joe muttered.

Janet Johnson gripped the steering wheel tighter and forced herself to take deep breaths. Although she hadn't recognized the people in the other car, she'd been unnerved by the close call. Until that moment, she hadn't realized how keyed up she was. She couldn't afford to be careless now. It could ruin everything, and she had come so close—closer than she'd ever dreamed possible. With any luck, Dick could be hers again, but she had to play her cards right.

Parking three blocks away, she started walking, her heels clicking purposefully with each step. She'd dressed carefully, certain that the impression she made would be all-important. She wanted to look like an attractive, but very responsible, young woman doing her civic duty to expose corruption when she discovered it. She had chosen a gray wool dress with a shawl collar, black patent pumps, and her best tweed coat for the effect. Clutched against her chest was a thick manila envelope containing such explosive information that Kathy Grant would rue the day she ever dared come back to Springfield, Janet thought smugly.

Arlo Thomas had been worth the steep fee he charged, and now that she had the evidence, she intended to use it so cleverly that nobody—least of all Dick—would suspect where it had come from.

Janet had never met the private investigator she'd hired. In fact, since all their correspondence had been by mail, she'd never even spoken to him until he called two weeks ago. Janet had been scared just hearing his voice. He sounded so rough and uncouth, she imagined him doing much more than twisting arms to get what he wanted. Her heart beat faster just remembering that unexpected call. The phone had rung at dawn, arousing her from a vivid dream of being with Dick. In her sleep he'd come back to her, desiring her so intensely he couldn't control himself. Marriage to Kathy had only whetted his appetite for her. Janet groped for the phone, groggy with sleep and hungry for the love that had been stolen away from her. She half-expected it to be Dick. Instead, the voice sounded coarse and threatening.

Thomas wanted more money—twice the retainer she'd already sent him. At first, Janet refused. She was already beginning to regret the madness that had impelled her to hire him sight unseen in the first place. She couldn't afford the money she'd already sent him. Another big payment was out of the question. It would empty her savings account, leaving her with nothing. But Thomas persisted. His voice alternately wheedling, then menacing and demanding, frightened her so much that in the end she reluctantly agreed, mostly because she didn't have the courage to refuse. What information could he possibly possess worth the price he was exacting? In her jealousy and anger, Janet feared that she'd put herself in the ruthless hands of an extortionist. But now that she had the information, she was sure that it was worth every cent she'd paid.

Glancing cautiously around her to make sure no one saw her enter, Janet slipped through the wide glass doors of the daily *Banner*. In the brief phone conversation she'd had with the city editor, she'd been assured that her confidence would be respected if the newspaper decided to use the information she had. But the editor insisted on seeing it himself before making any promises.

Ever since Kathy had come home, Janet had suspected that she was hiding some sordid little secret. But the truth was more explosive—and more shocking—than she'd ever imagined. Kathy wasn't guilty only of a previous marriage, but of ties to organized crime, a hit-and-run accident, and possibly even murder.

Janet was still reeling from her unexpected discoveries as she pulled a chair close to the city editor's desk and opened the manila envelope. She'd never been in a newspaper city room before, and its vast size, starkness, and banks of typewriters seemed intimidating at first. But, encouraged by the editor's obvious interest, she soon warmed to her story. Leaning nearer so that her dark hair just brushed his cheek, she revealed every damning detail that Arlo Thomas had supplied. The editor listened intently, his myopic eyes gleaming from behind his thick-rimmed glasses. He was already writing the sensational story in his head, picturing the front page layout—the big black banner headline above a picture of the mysterious Mrs. Lang.

"Is she pretty?" he broke in abruptly.

"I suppose you could say so," Janet admitted grudgingly.

"As pretty as you?" he pressed, considering her frankly.

A knowing, satisfied smile spread across Janet's face. She was more confident with every second that her revelations would be the talk of Springfield by morning.

Chapter Twelve

Banner Headlines

Stifling a yawn, Joe ambled down the familiar aisle of the *Banner* city room. It was just seven o'clock. The first two morning editions were already on the stands and only a skeletal staff remained on duty to make any changes in the final editions. They were all young reporters, people he scarcely knew who had joined the staff during his protracted leave of absence. Joe wasn't usually in the office until mid-morning, but Larry Powell had asked him to come in. The request had sounded so urgent that Joe didn't complain about the time.

" 'Morning, Larry!" he called, stepping into the glass-enclosed cubicle at the rear of the cavernous city room that served as the managing editor's office. "What are you so bright-eyed and bushy-tailed about? You look like your best friend just died." Joe settled casually on the edge of the desk and eyed the managing editor with easy camaraderie. A lot had changed at the *Banner*; many of Joe's old cronies had moved on. But, he thought fondly, Larry Powell just kept rolling along like Old Man River.

Larry squirmed uncomfortably. He was a small, round man with dark-framed glasses too heavy for his face. He took them off, rubbed his eyes with his fists, and put them on again. Joe's aim was uncomfortably close.

"Almost," he mumbled disconcertedly. "Let's say, I hope a good friendship won't die."

Joe looked at him curiously. "What's up, Larry?" he inquired, ready to help his friend out if he could.

"You're not going to like what I have to tell you," Larry began awkwardly.

"Well, there's nothing new about that," Joe bantered.

"Don't bank on it, my friend," Larry warned. "Here. I want you to read this—and you'd better sit down before you do." He thrust a galley proof across the desk.

A thirty-point headline, black as mourning, confronted Joe. "MISSING WIFE OF N.Y. PUBLISHER DISCOVERED IN SPRINGFIELD." Below it the story began:

"Mrs. Robert Lang, who disappeared from the scene of an auto accident in New York in which her husband, an internationally renowned publisher, was killed, has been discovered living in Springfield, an informed source revealed to the *Banner* in an exclusive interview. Mrs. Lang has remarried and resides on Springview Avenue with her new husband, Dr. Richard Grant, Jr., a surgeon at Cedars Hospital.

"At the time of the accident, Lang & Co., long considered one of the most prestigious book publishing houses in the country, was under investigation as a front for organized crime. The allegations of mob connections shocked the book industry.

"Speculation about the case suggests the fatal auto collision may not have been accidental. Sources close to the investigation believe that the elusive Mrs. Lang may have set her husband up for a gangland murder. The District Attorney, when contacted by the *Banner* last night, vowed to make a full-scale investigation.

"Kathy Lang Grant grew up in Springfield. She is the daughter of Joseph Roberts, for many years an investigative reporter with this newspaper. . . ."

Joe could feel his chest constrict as he read. The story went on to discuss Kathy's glamorous life in New York, shady connections, and sudden disappearance, but he'd seen enough. All at once, his clothes seemed too tight. His tie was choking him. His breath came in short gasps. He had to fight the urge to rip open his collar. He clasped his hands together to hold them from his throat. They were cold and clammy. He felt as if he were strangling, but he knew better this time. It was his heart betraying him again. He tossed the paper down on Larry's desk, his stomach churning in disgust.

"You're not going to run that drivel, are you?" He tried to hold his fury in check, but the words came out in a grating cry.

Larry played nervously with a blue pencil. He couldn't look at Joe. "It's already gone to press—lead story.''

"Well, stop the damn presses, then,'' he ground out harshly.

"I'm sorry, Joe. It's a sensational story. We made it the lead in every edition this morning. If we didn't pick it up, someone else would, and it's right in our own backyard,'' he finished lamely.

"It's trash and you know it. You haven't even talked to Kathy.''

"We will—today.''

"I thought the *Banner* prided itself on always printing both sides of every story,'' Joe charged angrily.

Larry looked away, embarrassed. "We will, tomorrow. Times change. We've got this hotshot new city editor—the publisher's fair-haired boy. . . .''

"I know all that,'' Joe interrupted hotly. "I work here too, remember. But he doesn't know what he's doing!''

"The new editor's ideas come from a different breed—''

"Damn the new editor.'' Joe's clenched fist came pounding down on the metal desk. "Are you the managing editor or aren't you?'' He couldn't believe that the *Banner*, the paper where he'd worked most of his life, would stab him in the back like this. Gripping the edge of the desk, he fought a dangerous battle with himself to check the surge of rage bursting inside him.

The clear, rational part of his brain that had earned him a reputation as one of the finest investigative reporters in the business warned him to go slow. There could be a solid story beneath all the hysterical charges. But it hadn't been checked through or verified. Joe smelled the vindictive hand of an informer. Joe had used tipsters, too, to get a lead on a story, but he'd never published any information they had handed to him unless he could verify it independently.

No such close checking—in fact, no checking at all—had gone into this report. How could a young girl like Kathy have such a spiteful enemy? Who despised her enough to slander her like this? Certainly no one in Springfield, he felt sure, but in New York . . . ? Kathy's life in New York was a total blank. With an ominous premonition of disaster, Joe realized that for all he knew, the allegations could be true.

With his heart attack, Kathy's wedding, and then the new baby coming, there had never been time to talk to Kathy about New York. Joe thought regretfully that he should have made the time. But certainly, if Kathy had been in trouble, she would have come to him. She always had. There were no barriers between them, he assured himself confidently, then he stopped. No barriers except Meta. Had Kathy been calling out to him for help when she'd insisted on bringing Robin home to him instead of to Dick?

Joe's rational mind rushed on, probing and questioning. But it couldn't overwhelm the furious might of his emotions. He finally lashed out.

"Who the hell is your informed source? That's all I want from you."

Larry squirmed. "You know I can't violate a confidence."

"Remember me? Joe Roberts. For fifteen years I've broken my back for this paper. You're talking to me—man to man."

"A confidential source . . . it would be unethical," Larry hedged.

"Unethical!" Joe protested. "What the hell is running a piece of trash like this—Bible history?"

"Don't get excited, Joe," Larry pleaded helplessly. "Remember your heart."

Joe bent over the desk until he was only inches from the other man's face and stabbed a finger at the picture of Kathy that filled two columns of newspaper space. "That's my heart, right there. And you're tearing it apart with your bare hands."

Larry pulled back, frightened by the depths of Joe's passion. "I honestly wish I didn't have to run the story," he wheedled, "but you know how circulation has been dropping. A story like this. . . . "

"Sure. I know." Joe spat each word contemptuously in the other man's face. "Anything for the almighty dollar. Well, you've got my resignation as of ten minutes ago, *and* a libel suit on your hands that will give you a hell of a lot more to worry about than circulation. That way there'll be no conflict of interest when I nail your hide to City Hall."

A warning spark flickered in Larry Powell's eyes. "Not this time, Joe" he cautioned. "I think you should have a little talk with your daughter first."

*   *   *

Helping himself liberally to the maple syrup, Dr. Grant, Sr., tackled the heap of French toast that the maid had placed in front of him and opened the morning paper. The morning was blessedly still. Laura hadn't come downstairs yet. The French toast was browned exactly to his liking, and for once he didn't have a seven-thirty operation. He was just thinking how he could enjoy his breakfast leisurely when he saw the *Banner* headline.

The syrup stuck in his throat. "For Chrissake!" he choked. Slamming the paper down on the table, upsetting his coffee cup, he charged to the phone. The maid, who'd been hovering curiously by the kitchen door, rushed to clean up the mess.

"I'm sorry, Doctor," she began.

He turned on her wrathfully. "I won't have you cowering around here, listening at keyholes. If I catch you at it, you'll be out the door," he bellowed. "And another thing. Don't believe everything you read."

She started to answer his charges, but he brushed her denials aside. Bristling with uncontrollable rage, he started to dial.

Dick was just closing his apartment door when the telephone rang. He didn't want to take time to go back for it, then, thinking it might be Kathy, he changed his mind.

His father's angry snarl was so loud it filled the room. "Get over here on the double!"

Dick's whole body tensed at the sound of his father's voice. "What's the matter, Dad?" he asked as calmly as he could.

"That's what you're going to tell me as soon as you get over here," his father barked.

"I'll see you in the hospital, Dad. I'm operating in twenty minutes." Dick forced his voice to remain even, determined not to rise to his father's bait this time.

"Reschedule it."

"I can't," Dick protested.

"You can and you will. That's an order. Or I'll do it for you." Dr. Grant shouted and slammed down the receiver before his son could reply.

For a long moment, Dick stood clenching the dead phone, his temper flaring impotently. Then, reluctantly, he dialed Cedars Hospital.

Laura Grant was draped over the breakfast table in an attitude of dramatic despair, her ice-blue negligee rippling over her like lake water, when Dick arrived. His father was pacing the room. At every giant stride, he slapped his empty hand with the offending, coffee-stained newspaper.

" 'Morning, Mother." Dick bent over to kiss Laura, who immediately burst into tears and covered her face with her napkin.

"Dad," Dick said in tense greeting. Choosing to ignore his mother's puzzling outburst, he went to shake hands with his father. "You wanted me?"

"I take it you haven't read the paper this morning." Dr. Grant slammed the paper into Dick's outstretched hand.

"Not yet," he admitted guardedly.

"Well, you'd better," his father snorted.

"Not so loud, Richard," Laura wailed. "The help will hear you."

"They don't have to hear me," he snapped back. "They've got eyes. They can read, too."

As his parents vented their anger and embarrassment on each other, Dick glanced at the paper which had been folded back into quarters, and instinctively touched his breast pocket. Kathy's face smiled up at him, exactly as she looked in the high school graduation picture he always carried in his wallet. She was always smiling then. Now she rarely did, he thought wistfully, as his eyes traveled to the accompanying story.

The shocking words leaped off the page at him. He felt as if he were being attacked. His knees buckled; his head swam. Abruptly, Dick sat down, still staring at the printed page. His mouth tasted like gravel. Until that moment, Dick had attributed Kathy's peculiar behavior to postpartum depression.

"We'll demand a retraction on the front page. You'll deny everything, of course," his mother was sobbing. "Your father has already talked to his lawyers. We'll sue the *Banner*. Oh, I always told you not to get mixed up with those people. No good would come of it. They're not our kind. The wedding was shameful enough— then the child, and now this. How will I ever be able to show my face in Springfield again? We'll have to sell the house. Everything your father worked for is destroyed! The scandal. . . ." Laura wailed and flung her face down on the table.

Dick listened and watched numbly. Every

detail of the scene was magnified in his mind, but the central facts eluded his grasp. His brain stalled. All he could think of was the way his mother looked. He didn't remember ever seeing her disheveled before. The sight seemed as horrifying as the words he read. He couldn't digest them. He couldn't even focus his mind on Kathy and Robin.

"For Chrissake, shut up, Laura," Dr. Grant bellowed. "I want to hear what Dick has to say about this." Looming over his son, he waited menacingly for an explanation.

But Dick only stared at the paper, rereading the damning words until the stark, black-and-white letters dissolved on the page.

"Speak!" his father roared.

The angry shout triggered another bout of sobbing from Laura.

Dick tried to answer. His lips formed words but no sound came out. Clearing his throat, he tried again. "I have nothing to say."

"Nothing to say!" Dr. Grant exploded furiously. "Your wife may be wanted for murder and you have nothing to say?"

"Not until I talk to Kathy. I'm sure there's some explanation," he murmured weakly. "Something simple . . . a mix-up. . . ."

"How could a sordid story like that get in if she didn't want it to? Her father works for the goddamn paper, doesn't he?" Dr. Grant demanded.

Dick nodded mutely. He didn't want to think about why Kathy would do that to him. He didn't want to think of her making love to another man, even though he knew she had. But he couldn't erase the sickeningly vivid pictures that invaded his mind.

"Think of the scandal!" Laura wept. "The shame. Murder and mobsters. . . ."

Dick staggered to his feet. "Stop it! Stop it, both of you," he cried. "You've already tried and convicted Kathy before you even know what she has to say. It may be all lies," he accused, "but you've always wanted to think the worst of her."

"Where do you think you're going?" his father challenged as Dick stumbled blindly toward the door.

"To Kathy. I don't want her to see this alone. What if they're vicious lies?" he cried. But the hope was only in his words, not in his heart.

From sublime happiness, Dick felt cast overnight into rage and despair. And what he didn't suspect was that the worst was yet to come.

From his parents' home, Dick drove directly across town to the Roberts'. He knew only one thing with certainty. He needed desperately to have Kathy tell him that the story was a lie. All lies. But as he turned into the cul-de-sac where the Roberts' familiar brick house stood, the full impact of the story hit him. Both sides of the semicircular drive were lined bumper to bumper with cars. Warily, he inched forward. The Roberts' front yard resembled an armed camp; a swarm of people wielding notebooks and cameras littered the lawn. One of the reporters recognized his car, and instantly the curious horde turned and rushed toward the street, bombarding him with questions.

Dick slammed his foot on the gas and shot forward, scattering people like flies. Grasping the steering wheel so tightly his knuckles shone like bleached bones, he headed back to his own apartment. If he couldn't see Kathy, at least he could talk to her on the phone. But Dick didn't even slow down when he reached his own apartment. Reporters and photographers stood guard there, too, waiting to corner him. He sped toward downtown Springfield and pulled up beside the first pay phone he saw. Glancing around, afraid he might have been followed, he dialed the Roberts' number. The busy signal blared like a mockery. He waited, watching the second hand on his watch make the eternal progression from one to twelve, then tried again, and again.

Defeated, Dick climbed back into the car, wishing he'd wake up and find the shattering day only a nightmare. It had been the longest morning of his life, and it was still only ten minutes to ten. He could make it to the hospital if he hurried. The operation he'd rescheduled was a routine procedure. He could do it and then try Kathy again from the hospital.

Dick wavered. How could he face the staff of Cedars today? Everything in him cried out to grab Kathy and Robin and run away until the hideous nightmare was over. But if he did, it would be tantamount to admitting he believed the newspaper charges. Stubbornly, he turned the car around and headed back toward the hospital.

Wheeling through the wrought-iron gates,

Dick half expected to be accosted by waiting reporters, but the parking lot was empty. There was no one in sight except the security guard. Ducking in a side entrance, he took the emergency elevator directly to the operating room floor. Usually he had a cheerful word for everyone, but this morning the rigid, forbidding cast of his face served warning not to approach him. Ignoring the curiosity he saw reflected on every face, he scrubbed and operated in unrelenting silence that was interrupted only when he had to issue an order. As soon as the last suture was tied, he shed his surgical gown and retreated to the emptiness of his father's private office. Dr. Richard Grant, Sr., had not shown his face at the hospital all morning.

Dick slumped in the chair and tried Kathy again. He was still holding the receiver, listening helplessly to the busy signal, when there was a soft rap on the door and the knob turned.

"I thought I'd find you here," Janet Johnson said, slipping in before he had a chance to protest.

He sighed in exasperation, his emotions too depleted to retort angrily. "If you don't mind, Janet, I'd like to be alone."

"I know the feeling," she murmured sympathetically and closed the door behind her. "It must be terribly hard to have your personal life raked through the public press."

"I'd rather not discuss it, if you don't mind," he replied thinly.

"I know," she soothed. Her voice was like salve. "I won't stay. It's just . . . well. . . ." She lowered her eyes, hesitating. "I've been wanting to say something to let you know how sorry I am ever since I saw Robin." She spoke haltingly, almost shyly, only glancing up surreptitiously to gauge Dick's reaction. "I can imagine what a shock it must have been—thinking all along that she was yours, and then seeing. . . . Well, you know what I mean. And now this business on top of it. We all think you've been downright noble about it. Any other man—"

"What are you talking about, Janet?" Dick's strained voice echoed with intensity.

Clasping and unclasping her hands nervously, Janet moved over to the window and stared out. In a few weeks, the full flower of spring would resurrect the land from winter bleakness. "You know," she hesitated. "I mean about Robin being only one month early, instead of three as we had all expected."

The blood drained from Dick's face, leaving it as white as a hospital gown. "You're crazy," he accused wildly. "You don't know what you're talking about."

Janet looked up at him with wide, innocent eyes. "Of course I'm not an expert on obstetrics, but Peggy Regan is. She's the one who told me. And if anyone should know, she should."

Dick had been struggling heroically to keep from believing what he'd read in the paper. Now Janet's revelation hit him with the force of a bombshell.

"No! No! I won't listen." He leaped up, wild-eyed.

"Wait!" Janet shouted, but Dick was already

out the door, running down the hall with only one thought in mind.

"Kathy! Kathy!"

He had to reach her somehow, to put an end to the vicious accusations that were murdering their love. Once he reached the safety of his car, Dick drove like a man possessed, without thought to a destination. There was no place he could go safely, and so he sped on, stopping only to call Kathy again, and again, and again. And each time, he was defeated by the implacable beep of the busy signal.

When he finally managed to get through, it was Meta's voice, tense and guarded, that answered.

"Roberts' residence," she said curtly on the first ring.

"Meta," Dick gasped, "I've got to talk to Kathy."

He heard her inhale sharply. "Where are you?"

"I don't know," he stammered. "On the road somewhere. I've just been driving. I can't go home."

"Reporters there, too?"

"Not as many as at your place, but enough."

A short, bitter laugh jarred the line. "You're locked out, and we're locked in. Prisoners in our own home. Joe quit the paper this morning."

"Your three minutes are up," the nasal voice of an operator interrupted.

"I've got to talk to Kathy," Dick shouted, as if speaking louder would prevent the connection from breaking off.

"You can't," Meta answered more harshly than she'd intended. "She won't talk to anyone. She and Joe have been holed up in the den all morning, leaving me to man the phones, deal with the press, the D.A., and the insufferably curious."

"You've got to make her," Dick pleaded in a strangled voice.

"Please deposit five cents more or your call will be terminated," droned the operator, impervious to the human drama being enacted over miles of electrical wire.

The phone was silent. "Meta!" Dick cried, afraid he'd been abandoned.

"Maybe Joe can get her to talk to you." Meta's voice sounded even more strained. "Hold on."

Dick reached in his pocket for change and tried to insert a coin, but he was so nervous he fumbled. Just as he fit the coin in the slot, the phone went dead. He hung up and dialed again. Only the busy signal answered. Dropping the receiver, Dick slumped in the phone booth and wept.

Chapter Thirteen

A Friend in Need

Even though the D.A.'s investigation was floundering for lack of evidence, the newspaper attack continued, and Meta found herself caught in the crossfire. The press raked up every bit of scandal it could—including Meta's seamy past and sensational murder trial—and not even Joe could do anything to stop it. Tensions in the Roberts' home were almost unbearable. Although Meta understood what Kathy was going through since she'd experienced much of the same pain herself, she was furious at having her past dredged up again for the whole of Springfield to gossip about.

From the secluded motel where he'd holed up, Dick read every paper and listened to every radio broadcast. Fear of the bitter truths that he couldn't accept prevented him from trying to call Kathy again or from returning to Springfield. He could hide, but he could never escape the love that both devoured and tortured him. An innocent wife would have been waiting by the telephone for his call, instead of leaving orders that she wouldn't talk to her husband.

Whenever he shut his eyes, he saw Robin and Kathy. If he tried to sleep, they claimed his dreams. Denied even the comfort and momentary oblivion of a sound sleep, Dick thrashed on the motel bed that was too big for one person to sleep in without feeling abandoned. The radio invaded his restless slumber.

A saccharine voice, pitched low, was chattering as though the speaker were privy to the intimate details of his life. "Apparently, Dick Grant, paramour and now husband number two to suspected murder-mate Kathy Lang, believes the better part of valor is desertion. No one has glimpsed hide nor hair of the young doctor since the sensational story broke five days ago. He hasn't been home—that's certain—and he hasn't visited his patients, either. The staff of Cedars Hospital is as mystified as we are about the whereabouts of the usually conscientious young surgeon who, you remember, is none other than the son of the chief of surgery.

"The senior Dr. Grant is keeping a stony silence on the question of his son's whereabouts, and his wife is off on a very timely vacation at an undisclosed beach resort. Even the tropical sun, presumably, isn't as hot as the Lang-Grant imbroglio. Has young Dr. Grant found an angel of mercy to minister to his woes? Has calculating Kathy done him in, too? Or has the intrepid doctor simply turned tail and run? Tune in tomorrow for more clues to Dr. Dick's mysterious disappearance."

Dick lay as rigid as a statue until darkness fell and then the sun rose again. It had never occurred to him that by trying to escape, he might be adding fuel to the charges against Kathy. Early in the morning, he called home.

His father himself answered, barking gruffly into the phone, "Where in hell are you? Your mother's been frantic, calling hourly to find out if I've heard from you."

"In a motel, about fifty miles south of Springfield."

"Good. Stay there until this whole dirty business blows over."

Dick thought he detected both worry and relief in his father's voice. "I think I should come back and talk to Kathy. I want to know if I can get into the Roberts' house or if the horde of reporters is still camped out."

"My lawyers are going to do that for you." Dr. Grant brushed aside the suggestion as if it were inconsequential. "Do you want them to demand the kid?"

"What do you mean?" Dick started. In less than a week, he seemed to have lost all control of his life.

"We'll charge that little snit with being an unfit mother, if you want. . . ."

"No!" Dick screamed into the receiver. "Don't do anything. It's my life and my wife. I'm coming home."

He gripped the phone long after he'd hung up on his father, then slowly lifted the receiver again and dialed the number for Cedars Hospital. It was a call he knew he should have made days before—the moment Janet had paralyzed him with her stunning revelation.

Peggy Regan's crisp, professional voice was met with heavy silence. Then, finally, Dick spoke, framing the question he hadn't dared to ask.

"Peggy, I have to know. . . . It's about Robin." Dick's voice sounded alien to his own ears.

"Has something happened to her?"

Peggy's concern was as palpable as the room around him. "No. It's not that." Silence yawned again, unbridgeable.

"Dick, you sound so strange," Peggy began tentatively. "Where are you?"

He ignored her question. "How early was Robin?" he blurted in a sudden rush of words.

"Have you been talking to Kathy?" Peggy's voice came back bright and unflappable.

"No," he admitted. "Janet Johnson. Did you tell her that Robin was only one month premature?" he demanded.

"No." Her voice was sharper. "I never told her anything."

Dick exhaled as if he'd been holding his breath for the better part of a week. "Then it's not true?" he pressed, eager to believe that Janet had been wrong.

But Peggy hesitated. "Are you sure you really want to know?" she spoke slowly.

The color drained from his face and his answer came back in a rasping whisper. "I have to know."

"There's only one person who can tell you what you want to know, Dick, and it's not me," Peggy replied in a hollow voice.

"Kathy?" He sounded as if he were strangling on the name. "Everything comes back to Kathy."

"Wait, Dick," Peggy pleaded. "The truth isn't always the most important thing."

"Then what is?" Dick exploded.

"Love." The single word seemed to stretch across the line and balance in the distance between them. "Kathy loves you with all her heart. That's all I know, Dick."

Driving back to Springfield, Dick heard on the radio that the D.A. was dropping his investigation of Kathy due to lack of evidence. When he arrived at the Roberts' house, the reporters and photographers were packing up, already on the trail of a fresh lead. Only a few strays remained. Kathy's story was stale now, like yesterday's bread. Ignoring the pop of a lone flashbulb, Dick went into the familiar brick house, which suddenly felt inexplicably strange.

Outside, it was the first truly springlike day. Robins pecked at berries and the first crocuses in Meta's garden opened their purple petals. But inside the Roberts' home a bitter chill still prevailed.

Less than a week had passed since Kathy had seen Dick, but it might as well have been a lifetime. They sat on opposite sides of the living room, unable to bridge the guilt and mistrust that separated them. Kathy looked gaunt and ashen-faced in a prim navy dress with a white Peter Pan collar and cuffs. Dick didn't remember ever seeing it before. She hugged a throw pillow of vivid Venetian red in her arms—either for security or because they felt empty with nothing to cradle, he couldn't be sure. He ached to see Robin. But Joe had taken her out for a walk. Dick didn't know whether it was coincidence, or careful timing. He wasn't sure of anything anymore and he mistrusted everyone now.

He stared fixedly at Kathy with eyes that mirrored acute pain. His eyes were rimmed with dark circles. His mouth was set in a tight, determined line. He hadn't had a decent meal or a sound sleep since the first story broke, and it showed.

"I want the truth, Kathy," he demanded through clenched teeth. He was coiled like a spring at the edge of the seat, his hands gripping the cushion like a lifeline. "No lies, no tears, no sob stories. Is that clear?" His voice cut like a rapier thrust.

Kathy shivered at the unfamiliar sound and hugged the pillow closer. "You read the papers?" Her words weren't so much a question as a statement.

"Is there anyone in the state who hasn't?" he rasped.

"It's all true." She looked at him with a disconcerting directness, as if in her honesty she expected him to have some understanding or even mercy. "Except one thing. Bob Lang's death was an accident. I may have driven him to it, but I would never have been a party to his murder. Bob was good to me—I wish I could say the same for myself." She stopped to moisten her lips.

"I was very lonely when I went to New York,

and convinced that I could never come home."
She began her difficult story in a slow
monotone and held fast to it until the end, her
voice only faltering when she had to describe
the fatal accident.

In the kitchen, Meta lowered the soap opera
she'd been glued to and listened intently to the
drama unfolding in her living room. Her heart
went out to Dick. He deserved much better
than Kathy Roberts, she thought bitterly. But
Meta didn't try to fool herself. She was rooting
for Dick to win for her own sake, much more
than for his. At least then she'd have Kathy out
of the house.

Dick listened intently, too, in angry silence.
He'd expected Kathy to throw herself on his
mercy. Plead innocence. Defend herself with tears
and fresh promises. Instead, she was admitting
everything, sparing no detail, however painful,
in her confession.

"I've wanted to tell you for a long time. I
couldn't bear the lies any longer. That's why I
haven't gone home to you, not because I don't
love you, whatever you may think."

"How can you talk of love now? You used
me," he accused bitterly.

"Yes," she admitted. "I was desperate. But I
would have told you about Bob if you'd only
asked."

"No," he snapped. "You can't shift the
blame to me. My love was dumb as well as
blind. But I've wised up now. There's only one
person you've ever loved, and that's Kathy
Roberts. Your first husband was lucky. At least
he didn't have to live with the truth of what you

are too long. For once my parents were right. I never should have gotten mixed up with you. You have no morals, no honor, no conscience. Worst of all, you have no heart."

Kathy flinched at each charge as though he were striking her. "Then why does it ache so for you?" she murmured.

"If you really loved me, you would have trusted me. Instead you made a fool of me. I believed I had everything, when the truth was I had nothing. I thought I had married a girl I loved named Kathy Roberts. Instead I married another man's wife—Mrs. Robert Lang. And Robin. . . ." He faltered, overcome by emotions he couldn't contain. Whatever Kathy was or had done, he wanted desperately to have her swear that Robin was his. "What about Robin? I have another man's wife. Do I have another man's daughter as well?"

Their eyes met across an infinite gulf—an abyss of pain and ineffable sorrow. It seemed as if Dick's present and future were suspended. Then Kathy nodded bleakly. Her voice, when she answered, was a hollow whisper. "That's why I wanted to get married right away."

"Why couldn't you have been honest with me in the beginning, instead of deceiving me like this? I would have loved you anyway, even if I knew you'd been married before. Then Robin would be my own daughter now. Why did you do it? Did it give you some kind of perverse pleasure to watch me behave like a delirious fool over a baby you knew wasn't mine? I think I could forgive you everything, Kathy," he added bitterly, "except that. I was so excited about having a baby—*our* baby. And when she came, I was so proud. I love her so much." He broke off and covered his face in his hands.

"You're the only man I've ever loved—you have to believe that, Dick," Kathy pleaded, leaning forward as if to reach out to him if she dared. "I don't want to lose you."

A hard, sardonic laugh was her only answer. Dick stood up and towered over her menacingly. She shrank back in the chair. In all the years she'd known him, she'd never seen him lose his temper before. But violence consumed his face. The whole thrust of his body threatened it. He looked as though he could murder her with the tight-fisted hands held rigidly at his sides.

"How many men have fallen for that line?" he demanded bitterly.

"No," she tried to protest. "You're my husband—" But he cut her off sharply.

"As far as I'm concerned, we've never been married. I don't just want a divorce, I want an annulment," he spat contemptuously and turned away. "My father's lawyers will be calling you later today. You can fight me if you want, but—"

"No!" She looked up at him beseechingly, every fiber in her body begging him to understand. "I never wanted to hurt you, Dick. At least believe that. I thought we could be happy. The past was finished and—" Her voice broke and she turned her face away, unable to bear the loathing she saw reflected in his eyes.

"I'll do whatever you ask," Kathy agreed in a defeated whisper. "If only it will ease the pain

I've caused you."

Dick stared down at her, a tumult of emotions churning within him. His marriage was ending, and with it all his dreams. Kathy looked so forlorn, so pathetically vulnerable, so utterly defeated, that for an instant he wavered. The tilt of her chin, the sheen in her sad, violet eyes, the quiver of her lips overwhelmed him with the urge to gather her in his arms again—one more time—knowing he would never be able to hold her again, or taste the sweet mystery of her lips.

He started to reach out, one last time, then he caught himself. His mouth hardened cruelly. "There's just one more thing you should know, Kathy. In my eyes, Robin was never born. She doesn't exist."

Dick pulled into his driveway and got out of the car. No one barred his way or barked questions at him. No flashbulbs popped. Now that his marriage was over and his life in shambles, no one cared. A family had been destroyed, but nobody—not the voracious press or the insatiably curious public—wanted to know that, he thought bitterly as he pushed open the apartment door. He'd have to find a new place to live. He couldn't bear to stay here alone, without Kathy or Robin. Uncertainly, he looked around, feeling strangely disoriented. Then he realized what was wrong. The Christmas decorations that he'd put up with such love and excitement! He hadn't had the heart to take them down himself, but now they were gone. A bowl of fresh spring flowers was on the coffee table. In fact, the whole living room gleamed, as if it had been scrubbed and polished.

"Dick? Is that you?"

He started in surprise and whirled around. Janet Johnson was coming out of the kitchen, wiping her hands on a dish towel.

"What are you doing here?" he demanded, too surprised to be angry.

"I told you, if you ever needed a friend. . . . I thought now you might."

"How did you get in?"

"Your landlady. In case you don't remember, you've got a sister." She risked a smile. "Me. You look awful, Dick—like you just saw a ghost."

"I have, sort of," he admitted grudgingly.

Janet frowned. "What do you mean?"

"Kathy. I've been with her."

"All this time?" The question escaped before Janet had time to catch herself. She couldn't believe that Dick had gone back to Kathy even now. All her carefully laid plans were suddenly reduced to a pile of ashes.

"No," he snapped and began circling the room, stopping to finger familiar objects nervously. "I couldn't face what you told me about Robin so I ran away like the weak-bellied milksop my father always thought I was. I just got back a couple of hours ago." He looked around the room as if he were seeing it for the first time, so unfamiliar and so much brighter without the dried-out Christmas tree and crumbling laurel ropes. "Why did you do all this?"

"It wasn't much." She answered easily now that her worst fears had been put to rest. "Anything for a friend. We are still friends, Dick, aren't we?"

Dick looked genuinely surprised by her question. "Why wouldn't we be?"

"Well," she started uncertainly. "I was afraid after what I told you in the hospital. You know . . . people have been known to kill the messenger who brings the bad news."

"I don't blame you," he replied with touching innocence.

"I thought you knew, or I never would have said anything," Janet lied boldly.

He laughed harshly. "I guess I was the last person in Springfield to find out, wasn't I? You must all have had a hell of a laugh. See Kathy. See Dick. See Kathy pull strings. See dumb Dick dance. See dumb Dick make a fool of himself," he mocked.

"No, Dick," Janet insisted, shocked by the depth of his bitterness. "It wasn't like that at all—believe me. Everyone thought you knew and that you were putting up such a loyal front for Kathy's sake, to spare her embarrassment." She broke off, trying not to let her hatred show. "How *is* Kathy, anyhow?"

"Different," Dick hesitated, "and the same." In his mind's eye, he saw her as he'd left her, looking up at him imploringly with big liquid eyes like violet pools that even now he knew he could drown in, if he let his guard down for an instant. Was that love shining at him through the blur of her tears? "Oh, hell!" He gripped the mantelpiece and pounded his head against the hard edge. "What difference does it make? It's over between us—finished. We're getting an annulment. She agreed." He uttered each word as if the very process of speaking were painful to him.

Tossing the dish towel on a chair, Janet went to him and put her arms around his shoulder. Dick shuddered at the human touch and moved as if to brush her away, but Janet's tender words quieted him.

"I'm sorry, Dick," she said gently. "I know how much you loved Kathy, and little Robin."

"Everything you said was true. Everything! She admitted it." A dry sob shook his lean frame. "I should have listened to you all along. I've been such a fool." The tears of anger and loss he'd been fighting back overwhelmed him. Weeping helplessly, he turned and buried his face on her shoulder.

Janet folded him in her arms and held him fast. He was hers now—hers alone. The thrill of victory filled her, and she stroked Dick's hair, tightening her grip possessively. Her plan had worked more perfectly than she'd ever anticipated. There was no one to take Dick from her arms again.

"It doesn't have to be the end of anything except an adolescent fantasy," she murmured. "It can be the beginning of a new life. You tried to live out a boyhood dream. You had to grow up eventually—it was only a matter of time. Now it's over and you can go on to a new life, a new love that will grow and mature with you."

"Oh, Janet!" Dick's choked words were wrenched from his heart. "Why couldn't Kathy have been honest with me—straightforward like you are?"

Still stroking his hair soothingly, Janet looked at herself over his shoulder. She could see her glowing smile reflected in the wide mirror hung over the mantel. She was happy at last. And she was going to do everything she could to make Dick happier than he'd ever dreamed.

Gaze into the "Soap Opera future" with

YOU CAN NOW ORDER PREVIOUS TITLES OF SOAPS & SERIALS™ BOOKS BY MAIL

Just complete the order form and detach on the dotted line and send together with your check or money order payable to **SOAPS & SERIALS**:

SOAPS & SERIALS™
120 Brighton Road, Box 5201
Clifton, NJ 07015-5201

Please circle the books you wish to order:

THE YOUNG AND THE RESTLESS	BK # 1 2 3
DAYS OF OUR LIVES	1 2 3
GUIDING LIGHT	1 2 3
ANOTHER WORLD	1 2 3
AS THE WORLD TURNS	1 2 3
CAPITOL™	1 2 3
DALLAS™	1 2 3
KNOTS LANDING™	1 2 3

Each book is $2.50 ($3.25 in Canada).

Total number of books circled _____
  @ $2.50   ($3.25 Canada) $_____
Sales tax (CT residents only) $_____
Shipping and Handling $_____.95
Total payment enclosed (checks or
  money orders only) $_____
Name _____
Address _____ Apt. # _____
City _____
State _____ Zip _____
Telephone No. _____

GL3